MW00877880

Genie Daddy
SWAY!
WITHDRAWN
Dave Wolfe

Hart, Allysa

A Well Placed Wish

Cover Art by Allysa Hart at Allycat's Creations

Interior Formatting: Lee Ching with Under Cover Designs

This book is dedicated to five friends who have been holding my hand for the last couple of years. Through ups and downs, the good and the awful, these ladies have stood firm and proven to me we are more than just friends.

Lily, dude, there are not enough words to express the level of gratitude I have in my heart for you. You pushed me when no one else would and made me see myself in a whole new light. I have learned to be more confident in myself and to find my true happiness on the inside. You gave me courage when I thought I had nothing left, and you held me up with your unrelenting strength. Love ya bunches, Bossypants.

Lesley, from the day we started talking, we knew we were meant to be sisters. From playing the "What's your favorite?" game to long, tearful Skype sessions, you have remained constant. You love me when I need it and are not afraid to say the hard things. I think it was Kris who said it best, you are my soul mate. Love you, Sissy.

Rai, I am so so thankful to have met you. It is amazing to me how alike we are, and you help me realize I am not alone in a lot of my thoughts and feelings. You are upbeat and always cheering me on, and I can't wait to see your writing career blow up, because it's going to, because you are amazing. Love you, Twinsie.

Jenny, it's crazy to me how far we have come in such a short time. I can always count on you for anything! From taking care of my puppies to binge watching Netflix, you are the true epitome of a best friend. Love you, Bestie.

Delia, I could say so many things, but it comes down to one thing, support. You have helped me so much emotionally and spiritually and you are so selfless with your love. I appreciate you so much and look forward to each and every time we get to hang out. Love you, Deeds

Prologue

Two weeks before my twenty-third birthday, the day I would obtain financial freedom, and there I sat, on a dirty chair in a police station. I crossed one leg over the other and observed the hustle and bustle going on all around me. Uniformed officers answered phones, escorted people in handcuffs, and worked behind computers. There were a myriad of noises, and the smell of stale coffee floated through the air. It made my mouth water for a cup of the real heavenly elixir. I'd had a long night, and it had been well over an hour since he brought me in.

Same old song and dance. A new asshole cop pulls me over for driving slightly over the speed limit and gets his panties in a wad when I tell him who I am. I've never understood why each and every cop seemed to think they could do whatever the hell they wanted because they hid behind a badge. Well, he would learn like the rest of them had. The badge held no power over my family.

My father, the governor, owned the whole damn city. He came from old money. Old dirty money. For as far back as our family history had been traced, there had been a criminal enterprise attached. My ancestors were drug smugglers, flesh peddlers, and all around bad guys. My father was no better, and with the political clout, there was no stopping him. Not proud of this fact, I did like the money, so I took advantage of the perks of my last name.

I was untouchable. No one dared fuck with a Burelli.

And if they did, well, they were dealt with. I don't know how my father did it, and I truly didn't care, but people learned their place around us, and they learned quickly.

Daddy dearest was not a nice man, but I stayed out of his way, and he stayed out of mine. Except in times like this. Officer "Save the world one criminal at a time" had pulled me over for speeding and taken me into custody for driving under the influence. Coming home from a party where I had been drinking and participating in a little recreational drug use, I was sober. At least that's what I told the idiot. Just because I couldn't walk a straight line, he thought he knew better, but I would like to see him walk that line in my six-inch fuck me heels.

Vincent Burelli barged into the station with two of his bulky cronies at his back. Dressed in a three thousand dollar custom suit, every fiber of his being exuded wealth. I couldn't help but roll my eyes as each officer averted their eyes. They may as well have bowed at his feet. The pussies.

"Where's my daughter?"

I stood without a word and dusted off my dress. It was disgusting in that place, and I didn't deserve to be stuck there for so long. "I'm here, Daddy. I told them to let me go home, but officer "Do Right" here wouldn't listen to me."

I pointed at the man who brought me in, further sealing his fate. My father's eyes looked past me and pierced the flesh of the poor man. I felt a little sorry as I watched his bravado fade when he realized the magnitude of his mistake, however, it was the only way these jackasses would learn to leave me alone.

"Get in the car. I don't have time to deal with this."

I walked past him without a word, but no way was I getting in his car. He would get my keys, and I could leave and do whatever I damn well pleased. Two more weeks and I would be able to access my trust fund and get out of dodge. The city was not the only thing suffocating under my father's control.

The fresh air washed over me as I exited the building, and I took some deep breaths to cleanse my senses of the stuffy station. One of the goons followed me outside and stood sentry near me. I never kept track of their names because they rotated often, and I couldn't care less who they were. This one seemed bigger than the rest though. I took stock of his wide shoulders and large build. He looked like he could be an NFL linebacker. His face was scarred and covered in a thick beard. Not my type. I liked clean cut, slender pretty boys who could wine and dine me and show me a good time. Sighing deeply, I crossed my arms and waited for my keys. At that exact moment my entire life changed, permanently.

Chapter One

I scrunched my nose in disgust as I stood in front of my Aunt Mary's ancient antique shop. "It's only two weeks, Fi. You can do anything for two weeks." I grumbled, coaching myself as I dragged my oversize suitcase toward the entrance.

'I had only met Aunt Mary, my father's eldest—and estranged sister, once. Somehow, she had been the only one willing to take me in in the wake of the legal shit storm surrounding my father.

"There's my beautiful girl!" The door crashed open, revealing a barefoot Aunt Mary clad in black leggings and a multicolored kimono with a matching bandana tied around her head.

It was going to be a long two weeks.

"Well don't stand there like a bump on a log. Come, come! We have a lot of talking and work to do." She gestured with her arms impatiently. I took a deep breath and forced myself to walk toward her.

"I'm pretty tired. I kind of hoped I could take a hot bath and a nap"," I said, training my voice to convey the right mixture of weary hopefulness. Aunt Mary didn't fall for it.

"Ha! You can sleep when you're dead! And the hot water is out of commission, but I have been assured it will back on in a couple of days. There's something refreshing about starting your day with a cool brisk shower."

My jaw dropped open. *This woman is off her rocker*. "You know what. Aunt Mary? I don't want to invade your space. Maybe I should stay in a hotel."

"No can do, my dear girl. Your daddy has made a big mess, and there is no money for you. All his money is locked up, and you don't get a penny till you are twenty-three. By my calculations that means you are stuck with me for a little over two weeks."

She was right. Every cent and account and asset had been seized. If I didn't stay here, I'd be forced to stay in a shelter or beg one of my other family members for help. Burelli's don't beg, so I was stuck.

"Don't look so glum, dear. We are going to have such fun. I could use some help around here, and you could use some working."

"Work?" My tone was full of disgust as I regarded her with a weary side-eye, once again scanning the recesses of my brain for alternative options. "I don't work. It's summer, and I plan to enjoy myself."

Mary responded with a hard look. "Around here, we earn our keep. Work or go hungry. Simple. Come, come. The chores are not going to complete themselves." She grabbed one of my bags and gave me no choice but to follow as she headed toward the house.

Two weeks, two weeks, two weeks.

I barely held back a scowl as I followed her through the quaint shop. It was overcrowded and stuffed to capacity. I scanned the room trying to make some sense out of what I was seeing, but there really wasn't any sense of order to be had. The entire place was a clusterfuck of epic proportion. Dust tickled my nose, and I sneezed three times.

"See why I need some help. I can't keep this place clean on my own, and I can't afford to hire out. You came at the right time." Mary didn't stop, just kept on trucking up a narrow staircase to the apartment above the store.

Her apartment was the polar opposite of the mess downstairs. The furniture worn, but clean. Pictures hung artfully on the walls, and everything was neatly in its own place. "Your room is through there." Mary pointed to a flowery curtain and set my bag down in the middle of the floor.

"Gee thanks." I pushed aside the curtain and shook my head in disgust. The tiny space wasn't a room at all, but a closet! A small closet!

A single bed pushed into one corner and an old beat-up dresser with four drawers right next to it were all that fit in the tiny space. Dropping my bags onto the tiny patch of available carpet, I fell hard onto the bed.

"Fi!" Aunt Mary yelled from somewhere in the tiny apartment. "Come have a snack before we get to work. You need to have some energy in you."

"I ate on the plane!" I yelled back. I lied.

"Suit yourself. I will meet you downstairs in five minutes!"

I held my breath until I heard the apartment door shut and the footsteps fade, then I breathed a sigh of relief, kicked off my jeans, and made myself comfortable as I leaned back on the small but soft bed. It had been a long trying day. I deserved a nap.

The hunger pains hit, forcing me awake. I looked around in a daze, not sure if it was night or day since the cramped room had no clock or window. Leaving my pants on the floor, I made the short trek to the living room. The morning sun beamed through the large windows, raising the heat in the room by at least ten degrees.

"You make a habit of walking around in your panties, dear?"

"It's so hot in here! I would be naked if I could be. What's for breakfast?" I fanned myself as I sat down at the table and eyed Mary's bowl of cereal.

"You may have breakfast as soon as you finish up some chores. I gave you time to eat yesterday before you decided to sleep instead of helping me."

I rolled my eyes. Was she serious? "I get it. I'm sorry. I will help today. Can I eat first?"

"No, you may not. I told you my rules, and you made a choice. Choices have consequences in the real world, dearie, and the sooner you learn, the better off you will be"," she jabbed, not even looking up from the paper she read.

"Why did you want me here if you were going to be a mean old witch?" My legendary temper rose as I stood and glared at her. My penchant for tantrums was epic and well known.

"Be careful throwing the "W word around here. The preferred term is sorceress." Her response caused me to regard her with further disbelief.

"Preferred term? Are you fucking kidding me right now? You are a special kind of crazy, you know that? No wonder my father never wanted me to spend time with you."

Mary's whole body sagged in response to my low blow. Beyond hungry, pissed at the entire situation, I had no fucks to give. "There are many reasons your father chose to keep you from me. My being crazy was not among them, I assure you. Now if you are hungry, you may wash that sink full of dishes then pour yourself a bowl of cereal. Be downstairs in one hour, dressed and ready to work. Don't wear anything fancy; it will be covered in dust before the day is over." After that parting edict, she took her bowl to the sink and left the apartment.

I sat there stunned, staring at the closed door. What happened? I side-eyed the kitchen, wondering what evil lurked in the sink, the only saving grace, I couldn't see a pile over the counter. However, one dirty plate is one too many when you have never washed a dish in your life.

"Two weeks, Fi. It's only two weeks." The mantra played through my head as I limped through the chore and searched out the cereal. I would have preferred some fresh fruit, but all I could find were overripe bananas and what might have been a lemon at one point in time. It was now a yellow rock. I flung the fridge open and cringed when it revealed a half full quart of whole milk. Dry granola remained the only option I could see. "This place is going to be hell on my diet," I mumbled.

"Good, you could use some meat on those bones of yours." Mary came into the room carrying a dusty box that looked like it might crumble into dust at the slightest touch. "I figured since you already did a few dishes this morning, you could do a few more. This is antique china I got from an estate sale, so please be careful. If the entire set is here, it will sell for a pretty penny."

I half listened as Mary yammered on about fine china and other old crap while I continued snacking on my handful of granola. I preferred to start my mornings alone in my room with a large cup of coffee and a lot of silence. Our home staff knew better than to talk to me before noon.

"Is there coffee?" I asked, interrupting her mid-sentence. Coffee might make this day semi-bearable.

My hope disintegrated when Mary shook her head.

"Never did develop a taste for the stuff. I have tea bags and a kettle, somewhere."

"I guess that will do," I capitulated. "I just need caffeine."

"Sorry, dearie, but you won't find any of that here."

"Any of what, where exactly?" I asked carefully, praying my assumption was incorrect.

"Caffeine. I don't buy it. That stuff is addicting, and unless it occurs naturally in something, you won't find it in this house."

"Caffeine is natural! Oh my God." I crossed my arms on the table in front of me and dramatically flung my head onto them. "I. Am. In. Hell."

Mary had none of it. "Stop with the theatrics. You are a grown woman. Act like it. And, I suggest you get a move on, dearie. We have a lot to do."

"You keep saying that!" I moaned in exasperation. "I get it! You are excited to have a slave for a couple of weeks. Why does all of this have to be done now, anyway?"

"I'm not going to lie and say you didn't come at the perfect time, because you did, but you are not my slave. You are family who needed help, as I do." Her tone softened as she continued. "I need to get the shop back up and running, or I will be forced to sell. I was… sick for a while and could not keep up with maintenance. So if you would please finish your breakfast and help me, I would greatly appreciate it."

Again, Mary left the apartment without waiting for an answer. Her admission had made me feel slightly guilty about the way I had gone off, but God it had been a miserable twenty-four hours. I slunk back to my room to get ready. I checked my cell for the hundredth time that day, but the result was the same. No one bothered to check on me. As soon as everything went down with my father, I had been completely ostracized from the community. None of my "friends" even acknowledged my cry for help when I needed somewhere to stay, leaving me completely alone. I told myself it was fine, I didn't need anyone, but I wasn't a very good liar. I hoped my father would be exonerated so I could get into my bank account again and start a new life somewhere no one knew me or my family. Maybe I would even change my last name.

Elbow-deep in soapy water, scrubbing years of grime off each plate, I looked up when Mary came back for the fifth time in an hour to inform me, yet again, I was not doing the job correctly and made me start over for the sixth time. I flipped the bird at her retreating back and snarled down at the plate in my hand. Her persistence had paid off, however. I was mad as hell but more than determined to show her I could do it.

I worked tirelessly and stubbornly until my hands were raw and sore, my triceps aching from exhaustion, and my head pounding from the heat, but I was three dishes away from the finish line. Mary had brought up a few more boxes but had not added them to my pile, so I neared the end of this particular hell. God only knew what she planned to have me do next.

Mary suddenly appeared just as I dried the last dish. A proud smile swept across her face as she picked up a dry dish and held it up to the window, examining it with twinkling eyes. "These are beautiful. Look at the intricacies!"

"Oh, I saw each and every one of them as I picked the gunk out"," I grumbled, hiding a smile.

"Beautiful job my dear, thank you. How about some lunch?"

My stomach roared in response, giving me away. I was starving. "Yes, please."

"Great. Why don't you go out to the garden and get some vegetables, and I will put together some salad and sandwiches?"

I gaped at her. That put a whole new meaning to the phrase working for your supper. "Are you serious?"

"Nope, but the look on your face says you are about ready to kill me. Lighten up, dear. It was a joke. There is no garden. My fresh fruits and vegetables are delivered every couple of days." Mary laughed.

Shaking my head at her idea of a joke, I cleaned off my hands and pressed a wet towel to the back of my neck. "How can you stand this heat? You aren't even sweating."

"The shop is a lot cooler because there are more windows and we get a cross breeze. We can work together down there after lunch."

"Oh goody." Despite my dry response, the idea of a cross breeze of any sort sounded appealing after spending the morning in a virtual sauna.

"You could always do more dishes, dear." Mary pointed to the boxes, but I shook my head quickly.

"Working in the shop will be fine, thanks."

"Mmm hmm." Mary brought in a basket full of vegetables and began throwing together the most colorful salad I had ever seen. Mixed greens, carrots, bell peppers, radishes, cucumbers, purple onions, and cherry tomatoes all blended together to make a bountiful feast almost to pretty to eat. Almost.

"Ham or turkey?" Mary asked.

"Can I have a little of both? I will chop it up and put it in my salad."

"You may." Mary laid a couple of pieces on the plate and made herself a sandwich. "Help yourself." She gestured to the pile of food, and I sighed. Of course I had to make it myself.

"Sorry, dearie, no one here is going to wait on you. You have to learn some independence."

Two weeks, I reminded myself. Two long fucking weeks.

Chapter Two

Mary had not been lying. I found the temperature in the shop way more bearable than that of the apartment. I wondered if she would let me sleep down here. Mary rambled on about her assorted collections, but it all looked like trash to me, as I peered around in a daze, trying to follow her steady stream of chatter. Finally, she pointed to a corner near the back of the shop. "You can start there. I will start on the opposite side, and we will meet in the middle. Every inch of this place needs to be cleaned and organized. Remove any broken items you find and place them to the side. If you have a question about something, leave it where it is and I will look."

"What is all this crap? Do people really buy this stuff?" I stalled. It was barely noon, and we had already been working for hours. I wanted to sit and enjoy the cool breeze.

"The right people do, yes. My neighbor is always hounding me about selling things on the eBay or what have you, but there is something lost in that. I like interacting with people, telling them the stories behind pieces and hearing their tales in return. You can learn things you never imagined, just from listening."

The joy on her face as she spoke perplexed me, her passion for all her old crap obvious. I felt a stab of jealousy I didn't quite understand. Nothing in my life lit me up like that. Nothing made me as happy as Aunt Mary with her piles of crap. All I really did was spend money. Ninety percent of the time, I didn't even need the things I bought. My walk-in closet back home was full of things I had never worn, yet I kept buying more. If I wasn't careful, I would end up with a mess like the one in the shop. But I still wouldn't be happy

"Ready to start?"

"Ready as I will ever be." Another lie. I had missed most of Mary's instructions and had no clue what was trash and what wasn't. I grabbed one of the buckets of soapy water and went to the corner Aunt Mary had pointed out earlier. "Here goes nothing."

Starting with the top shelf, I took down each item, cleaned it, and set it to the side. When the shelf was empty I wiped it down and the old brick wall behind it. The bucket of water and rag I got dirty really fast, and I had to make multiple trips back and forth to the back room to retrieve clean water. Lugging the water back and forth was one of the hardest parts. The water would slosh over the sides and get all over me and the floor. I placed my steps carefully, avoiding the wet spots. *I'm going to slip and bust my ass on one of those puddles.* Putting my hands in the clean water was refreshing, but the muddy water made me want to hurl. I didn't even want to know what I smelled like, but it had to be rank.

Hours passed as we worked shelf by shelf. Tired, sweaty, and hungry, I paused to admire the fruits of my labor, filled with pride. I had never worked so hard—or, basically, at all—and seeing the progress felt good.

Mary came up behind me. "Well done! Look at you go. You keep at it and I will go whip us up some dinner. 'How's that sound?"

Wiping sweat from my face, I nodded. "Sounds great, but are you sure you don't need help with dinner?"

"Don't be silly. I wouldn't want to interrupt your progress. You need to catch up with me anyway." She gestured to the wall she had been cleaning, and it was almost finished.

"I guess I'm slow."

"You're doing great, and I am so proud. Finish this section and come get cleaned up."

When I turned back to the wall, my pleasure abated and frustration returned. I hated work, and I hated being dirty! Still, I determined to finish. Sighing, I grabbed a dusty glass bottle off the shelf and it hit the one next to it, creating a sort of a domino effect before crashing to the ground.

"Oops." I cringed and waited to see if Mary would hear the crash and come down. When she didn't appear, I sighed with relief. Time to find a broom. The back of the shop held a bathroom, a small room with a desk, potentially an office, and a closet. Of course, I found the broom in none of those places, because that might actually make a lick of sense. Growling, I collapsed onto a desk chair and gasped when it rolled backward and hit the wall behind me. A loud creaking sound startled me out of my seat, and I turned around to see a huge crack in the wall. No, it was a door.. A closet camouflaged by a large cork board overflowing with different documents. Curious, I pushed it open and shivered for a moment before stepping inside.

The space was dark and covered in cobwebs. I started to exit almost immediately, but in the back corner I spotted a small broom. It was the old style, the kind a child would use for a Halloween costume, but better than nothing. Swiping my hand back and forth in the air in front of me like some sort of ninja, I tried to keep the cobwebs from hitting my face. *I hate spiders.*

A small chain hung from the ceiling, and I tugged it.

Thankfully it still worked, and the room filled with a dim light. When I looked around, I found myself wishing for the darkness. Shallow shelves cluttered with marked jars and bottles of all shapes and sizes filled the walls. At least an inch of grime coated them. I picked up the bottle closest to me and wiped off the label.

"Love Potion?" *Are you kidding me?* Shaking my head, I rubbed my fingers over the label once more, clearing away the final layer of dust. Smoke began slowly seeping from the top of the bottle, and I dropped it, jumping back and falling to the ground in fear. *What the fuck?* The smoke cloud grew, filling the small room, until I could barely see in front of me. I crawled in a circle on the floor, trying to get my bearings as I searched for the exit. The air in the room swirled in a miniature tornado, sucking in all the smoke until the room cleared. In a backward crab walk, I moved as far as I could from the cloud that formed. I hit the wall and froze to the spot. One of the most beautiful men I had ever seen had magically materialized right before my eyes. No, there was no such thing as magic. This had to be some sort of trick. I looked around to see if Mary had somehow pranked me, but I remained alone in the room, save the purple muscled masterpiece created out of smoke.

Still on my hands and knees, I checked him out from head to… waist. He was only half a man. "A naked purple half man floating on a cloud. Am I dead?"

His eyes went from a trancelike state to traveling around the room and landing on me. They matched his body in color, but with such depth behind them. He stared at me for a moment before his gaze softened and his mouth tipped into a smirk.

"Is this how people greet genies in your time?"

His voice fell somewhere between a low rumble and a

growl. It vibrated through me, and I felt my body respond. The tingle started behind my ears and traveled lower, brushing my nipples and settling in my sex.

"Do you not speak?" He crossed his muscled arms over his chest and replaced the smirk with a full-mouthed smile. His white teeth shone bright against the dark purple of his lips. Soft, pillowy lips, from the looks of them. Oh God, why couldn't I talk? The necessary words would not form on my tongue. Neither of us moved, just stared each other. Millions of questions ran through my mind, but none of them came out. I had to focus on breathing I felt like I was going to pass out.

"Mary!" I didn't yell, but the name came out loud and surprised us both.

"Is that your name? Interesting."

I shook my head.

"Maybe you would like to stand?" He offered his hand in a gentlemanly gesture, but I couldn't take it. I threw myself backward, landed on my butt with a hard thud, and banged my head against the wall behind me, rattling the glass jars above my head. Dust flew everywhere, coating my sweat-soaked skin and clothes. The cloud floated backward slightly, giving me some space.

"You do not need to fear me. I am here to serve you."

Serve me? I shook my head back and forth hard to try to wake up from this crazy dream. Was it some sort of hallucination? "Y-you're not… you can't… you aren't real! I'm dreaming or something. Maybe I have heat stroke and am imagining someone saving me from this hell. Yeah, like a mirage." The concept sounded crazed even to my own ears, but what else could I say?

He looked around the room, "This does not appear to be hell."

"How would you know? You haven't even been here

five minutes." I looked around frantically for anything that would help me wake up. "Oh God, now I am arguing with it. I need something to drink. Something cold, with caffeine. I freakin wish I had an ice-cold Coke right now."

"Your wish is my command."

With a snap of his fingers, a frosty bottle of Coke appeared next to my hand, and I jumped away as if it were a spider about to attack.

"Is that not what you wished for?" His head tilted to the side like a confused puppy.

"I-I did but…" My head swiveled between him and the drink. *What the hell is going on?*

"Quite a modest first wish. I would be a bit more careful with the second one if I were you. You only get three, and I cannot control them, only you can. Any time you say 'I wish,' it will come to pass, with a few minor rules."

I sat stunned by the whole scene.

"I see you still do not believe. Pick it up. Refresh yourself."

I obeyed without question. His words were so strong, so commanding. I had never felt compelled to do anything I was told, not without a fight at least. I tried to open the bottle, but it wouldn't budge. The man snapped his fingers, and the cap flew off, landing on the floor with a ping and rolling around for a second before finally falling flat. I watched it the whole time, staring at the inanimate object until the coldness of the drink penetrated my haze and I set it down.

"You still do not believe?" He shook his head in disapproval before snapping his fingers once more. The coke floated from its place up to my mouth. "Open."

I parted my lips. The bottle tipped slowly, resting against my bottom lip as the liquid made its way to my taste buds. I moaned in delight and grabbed the bottle, tipping it farther, faster, then it was snatched away.

"Hey!" I wiped my mouth angrily and scrambled to my feet, chasing after my drink. Even when I was standing, his bulk dwarfed me, and technically he was only half a man, with only a cloud from the waist down. I took one step toward him and reached for his hand. "Give that back!"

"You need to drink slowly. Caffeinated beverages can expand in your esophagus and cause pain."

"I am a grown woman. I don't need you telling me what to do."

"You appear grown, I will agree, however, your actions are those of a spoiled child."

"You can't say that. You don't even know me." I pouted and turned away to hide my heated cheeks. He hadn't even introduced himself and already he was judging. Why was I so embarrassed? I knew I was spoiled, hell I loved it, but something about the way he said it made my heart ache.

His large hand engulfed my shoulder and turned my body to face him. "You are correct. I should not make such rash judgments. I have not spent an adequate amount of time getting to know you. You have my deepest apology for my misstep."

My eyes widened, and breath caught in my throat. He was apologizing? No one ever apologized. In my life, people got angry, went away, and came back when they could pretend nothing had ever happened. His hand still rested on my shoulder, and its warmth settled in my bones. Unable to help myself, I lifted my hand and placed it against his chest. Solid muscle. I felt compelled to run my hands up and down his entire torso, but that would be weird. This whole thing was weird.

"Now do I have your belief?"

My eyes left his chest and raised to meet his. "You talk funny."

A chuckle rumbled from somewhere deep and moved through my hand. My panties dampened instantly. *What the hell?*

"Yes, I know. That is one of the downfalls of spending years in my chambers. I revert to the speech I learned as a boy. Soon enough, I will sound as if I am from your time. What year is it?"

"2017."

His face turned pensive. "Twenty-eight years, then. I believe that is my shortest rest yet."

"You were in a wine bottle for twenty eight years?"

"I believe it is a bottle for potions, but yes."

"Where's your lamp? Aren't genies supposed to be in lamps?" It began to get easier to form questions, but this all still felt like a very weird dream I would wake up from at any moment.

He shook his head. "That is where we begin, but after the third wish of the one we serve, we are sent into the object representing their personal vice. I have resided in a mirror, a small coin, a multitude of places. Genie's do not take much space."

"So the person you served before now was..."

"She dabbled in the arts of witchcraft."

I gulped and looked again at the room we were in. "I need to get out of here."

He snapped his fingers and, suddenly, we stood outside, behind the shop. The fresh air penetrated my lungs, clearing out the stagnant air from that tiny room. I looked up at the genie again. "Thank you... I don't even know your name."

"Shame on me. I have not properly introduced myself. I am Callum."

"Callum," I whispered. His name felt natural on my lips. "Do you have a last name?"

"You are the first of my girls to ask that of me." His stunned look told me he spoke the truth.

"In my world, last names rule."

"How is that so?"

"Well, my name is Fiona Burelli. My father is a known powerhouse. That means no one goes against me, and I get what I want when I want it." I confidently relayed the information. If this was real and he planned to be serving me, he should know what to expect.

"That does not sound appealing."

"What? It's amazing."

"And if you are not fortunate enough to have a certain name?"

I shrugged, " I never really thought about it."

"You don't often consider others?" The realization he could make my feel two inches tall with a simple inquiry pissed me off. No one had ever instilled such a feeling in me, and I didn't like it. Not at all.

I turned away from him. "I consider people who mean something to me. Why do I need to worry about the whole world and its problems?" Damn that sounded lame. He made me uncomfortable, and I didn't know how to battle back. Sexy genie or not, no one got to hold power over Fiona Burelli, ever.

Callum stayed silent behind me, compounding my uneasiness..

"It's not like me living my life affects them anyway. I can't change who they are." That felt like a better argument.

"You cannot. However, how you treat them can make all the difference."

"How I treat them? We live in totally different worlds.

They don't come into mine, and I certainly don't go into theirs."

"No? The people who serve you, then. They are a part of your world, are they not?"

He made me spitting mad, "Who do you think you are, mother fucker? Seriously. Are you here to grant me wishes, or are you here to pass judgment about people you don't even know?"

"I pass no judgment except the one I have already apologized for. I cannot control that my inquiries create frustration within." His logical answers made it. Why does all this matter to you, anyway? It's not like we are friends. 'You're only here to give me stuff. So cut the questioning shit."

"Your language when you are upset leaves much to be desired." His glare gave me butterflies.

"My language is not your concern so, go fuck yourself."

His expression darkened, and I took a step away from him.

"You may assume, now, however, I warn you, the moment I am given the opportunity, you will find yourself being disciplined for your speech, among other things. Of this, I am certain."

My mouth fell open in shock. "Discipline? Are you serious?" I couldn't stop the nervous laughter from overflowing. "Y-you? Who do you think you are? I mean really! Discipline? Me? Not a chance in hell, buddy. My own father doesn't even discipline me."

"That explains more than any of the other nonsense you have spouted. Your father has done you a terrible injustice."

"Don't you dare speak of him!" I screamed, stomping my foot for good measure.

"You are the one who brought him into our conversation. I am permitted to comment. 'Fathers are commissioned to provide their children with loving discipline and guidance."

"Let me stop you right there. My father is not loving and never has been, so you can take your beliefs and shove them up your...umm," I paused as I took in the cloud encircling his waist and halted. I didn't have a comeback. "Ugh, whatever, never mind."

"Children require love from their daddies to grow and flourish, to thrive. I hold deep sorrow in my heart for the little girl inside you,"

The word "daddy" struck a chord, and I almost choked when I tried to swallow the lump forming in my throat. My eyes burned, but I refused to allow tears to spill. Averting my eyes, I admitted something I had never told anyone else. "I was never allowed to call him that."

Callum closed the gap between us and lifted my chin. I wanted to fight, but I was frozen to the spot. "Your behavior reflects your mistreatment. On behalf of all of mankind, I apologize for the way you have been treated. You hold deep hurt in your heart. It will destroy you one day if you do not learn to release it."

I took a step back. He already got too close, freeing emotions I didn't have time to deal with. He was supposed to be granting me wishes, not psychoanalyzing me. Time to call it a night before I unleashed the waterworks for real. "Yeah, well, thanks, I guess. I'm fine. I just learned to be tough and not care. It's not a big deal. I should go upstairs and see if dinner is ready. I'm hungry."

Callum shook his head and floated backward. "You, little girl, need a daddy."

And then, poof, he disappeared. All of a sudden I was back in the small room of the shop. Looking around, I spotted the bottle on the floor. Picking it up, I turned it upside down. Empty. I placed it back on the shelf and left out the secret door. His last words played over and over in my head. The only normal sounding sentence to come out of his mouth the entire conversation.

I put everything back the way I found it, completely forgetting what I had been doing back there in the first place. Trudging up the steep stairs to the apartment, I felt muscles ache I didn't even know I had.

I opened the door to see Aunt Mary looking into an open cabinet. No smell of food, no mess, nothing. "Did I miss dinner? I'm sorry I took so long I, umm, I got lost in my work." I lied through my teeth.

Mary looked at me, confusion etched in her face, "What are you talking about dear? I haven't even gotten started."

Impossible. I had been with Callum for at least thirty minutes, if not longer. Of course I couldn't tell her. *What the fuck is going on?*

Chapter Three

Still puzzled from the apparent slowing of time, I hopped in the shower while Mary whipped up a chicken casserole. The aroma made my mouth water, but when I emerged from the shower and peeked at the dish, I could tell it contained multiple ingredients I usually abstained from eating. My stomach growled, and I couldn't find any fucks to give about my diet.

We sat down and dug in, each lost in our own thoughts. Mine were stuck on Callum. I couldn't stop playing back his last words over and over in my mind. The little girl inside wanted to climb into his arms and beg him to be my daddy, but the grown woman wanted him naked on top of me, asking who my daddy was. The thoughts conflicted, but each side wanted him in her own way. Back home, men flocked to me like flies to honey. None of them affected me the way Callum had. And that scared the fuck out of me. Something called me to him, something completely out of my control. For God's sake, I didn't even know the man. Oh hell, he wasn't even human.

"I cooked, so you are on dish duty, dearie." Mary announced as she got up from the table and placed her plate in the sink. I sighed, but fair was fair, and I had no idea how to cook. At home, we had a chef who left ready-made meals in the fridge and freezer. I set the temperature and time and left the dirty dishes on the table, or I ate out.

Neither was an option in this place, so I resigned myself to having dish duty after every meal.

"After only twelve hours in detainment, Vincent Burelli has been released," the anchorman on the television announced, "because vital evidence had disappeared." Gasping loudly, I turned off the water, dried my hands, and moved closer to the television. Perched on the arm of the loveseat, I listened intently to what the man said about my father. "Our sources tell us a key witness and vital evidence have both disappeared. Burelli's team refuses to comment on the case."

I couldn't believe what I heard. My father was out, and he hadn't even called me. Stomping into my room, to find my cell phone. No texts, no messages, no emails, nothing. "That son-of-a-bitch!"

Mary followed me in. "Take a breath, sweetheart. Maybe he is tied up."

"Too tied up to fucking call his only daughter? I didn't know how to get a message to him, so he doesn't even know where I ended up. He doesn't know if I am okay, nothing! He doesn't know I am living in the middle of nowhere working for my meals. He's a selfish prick. I'm going to go home and tell him exactly what I think, then I'm going to get a credit card, stay in the nicest fucking hotel I can find, and live on his dime for two weeks. Then I am fucking gone. I will move away and never talk to him again, I swear!"

My aunt stayed quiet as I spouted all my anger and frustration. I knew some of the things I was saying could hurt her feelings, but she didn't acknowledge any of them. She was a silent supporter, exactly what I needed at the moment.

Throwing myself backward onto the bed, I covered my eyes with my arm and tried to hold in the tears.

"I hate his guts."

"I know the feeling," Mary admitted as she sat down on the side of the bed. "I know you are upset, and I know living here is not what you are used to. However, you are always welcome in my home. More than that, though, I like having you around."

"Sure you do, free slave labor"," I scoffed.

"The help is nice, but the company is nicer. I was looking forward to getting to know you for a few weeks. Bottom line, dear, I would be sad to see you leave."

It warmed me from the inside out. I had thrown attitude and rude remarks out at every turn, and yet, somehow, this woman actually wanted me around. "It's too late to go anywhere, anyway, so I guess I'm stuck, for tonight at least."

Mary chuckled and squeezed my leg, "Don't sound so excited. I might get the wrong idea about how you really feel."

I smiled and shook my head. 'I hadn't noticed how comfortable I felt in our relationship until that moment. We were raw and honest with each other. Neither willing to give in, yet it seemed to work.

"Get some sleep, dear. Tomorrow is another busy day." She kissed my cheek and left me alone with my thoughts. I got out of bed and opened my laptop, looking for a way to get home. At least 'I told myself so, but I wasn't ready to leave. This place may be a shithole, but it held a magnetism I couldn't ignore. And, Callum. Frustrated, I slammed the computer shut and threw myself onto the bed again. Closing my eyes, I tried to forget the world for a few hours.

"You, little girl, need a daddy," Callum's voice echoed.

"Yeah? Are you applying for the position?" I shot back with all of the sass I had.

Approaching me, he took my wrists in a tight hold, backed me against the wall, and pinned my hands above my head. "Consider me the only applicant, because no one touches what's mine. And you are most definitely mine."

With one hand holding me still, he used the other to lift my night shirt and expose my breasts. I took in a sharp breath as his thumb zeroed in on my nipple and teased. His eyes stayed trained on mine while he switched to the other breast, giving it the same attention. My eyes rolled to the back of my head, my breathing labored. Luckily, his hold stayed fast because when his gentle teasing turned to sharp pinches, my knees buckled.

His lips found my neck, and he chuckled, sending vibrations straight to my pussy. "My girl likes it rough, huh?"

I whimpered in need.

"Don't cry, baby. Daddy is going to put out that little fire. Be a good girl and keep your hands where I put them."

Nodding, I bit my lip as his eyes darkened.

"The correct answer is always, 'yes, Sir.'"

His edict sent another shiver through my body. "Yes, Sir"," I whispered right before he captured my lips in a toe-curling kiss. With his hands working my breasts and his lips laying claim to my mouth, all I could do was enjoy the ride. Wrapping my arms around his neck, I pulled him in, closer. I wanted to feel him against me, all of him. He released my mouth and breasts long enough to pull my shirt over my head and carry me to the bed. As soon as I was on my back, he secured my arms above my head again, knotting a soft fabric around my wrists. Never had a man taken charge of my body like this; I wouldn't have allowed it. But Callum didn't ask. He seized what he considered his, and he conquered it without the slightest hesitation.

Straddling my body, Callum sat up and raked me with his eyes. The look on his face was carnal. His fingers softly trailed from my hands down my arms, around my breasts and tickled down my sides, stopping at the lace of my panties. Taking hold of the seams on each side he gave a sharp tug and tore them off my body.

"Oh God"," I whimpered as they fluttered to the floor.

"That's just the beginning, my love." He engulfed one of my nipples with his mouth, sending a warm sensation straight to my clit. My back arched as I cried out for more. Callum didn't let me down. He latched onto my other nipple and bathed it with his tongue.

"Please. Please." I begged. For what, I didn't know, but I wasn't capable of anything else at the moment..

"Please what, sweetheart? What do you need from Daddy?"

"I need to come, please."

Callum smiled. "You beg so beautifully. I'm going to reward you. You may come when you are ready. As many times as you need to."

His tongue, teeth, and lips worked my entire body before settling at my core. "Are you ready?"

"Please." Closing my eyes, I rocked my head back and forth. I needed him so badly, it hurt.

My eyes flew open as a loud beeping noise filled the room, and I almost fell out of my small bed. Small bed? I was awake, and Callum was gone. "No! No no no! That's some fucked up shit."

The beeping began anew, coming from my phone. Seeing my asshole father's number raised my ire. Talk about bad timing. I shut the phone off and threw it in a drawer then lay back down, but sleep evaded me. I tingled from head to toe, and all I could think about was getting back to sleep so Callum could finish what he started. Unfortunately, I heard Mary moving around in the other room, signaling it would soon be time to get up. Frustration washed over me, and I wanted to cry. Instead I turned over into my pillow and screamed at the top of my lungs.

"Are you okay in there, dear?" Mary called out.

Okay? No, not okay. I was horny as fuck, with no way to remedy it. No privacy, and no man. Anger rose in my chest, and I swore the next time I saw that purple pain in the ass, I would kick him in the balls.

"I'm fine!" I returned.

I wasn't fine. I was sweaty and horny and alone. The only feasible remedy I had was a cold shower and a giant coffee. I groaned as I remembered my location. The cold shower was a sure thing, but the coffee a hopeless case. What I wouldn't give for an iced latte.

Chapter Four

Standing in the shop, I looked at the broken bottle gotten hadn't cleaned up the night before. Every muscle in my body ached, and seeing all of the work that still needed to be done made me want to cry. What had I done so awful as to make me deserve this? Last I checked, being born wealthy was not a punishable crime.

"Staring at the wall is not going to get the job done, you know",," Mary said from somewhere behind me. The last straw. My morning had been bad enough, and I wasn't in the mood for her shit.

My face heated, and I turned on her. "I'm done. Finished! This entire store is a piece of shit. I have no fucks to give if it is foreclosed upon. It's full of trash, and making it clean trash is not going to accomplish anything. You are wasting my time and your own. Get a fucking life!" Releasing my frustration helped, somewhat, and I refused to let her defeated expression affect me. Stomping to the door, I flung it open and left without another word.

The town was small, one of those places you drive through and never stay, but Mary constantly boasted about how much it had to offer. Without chain stores or restaurants, really there was nowhere I could go to gain a feeling of home, and I didn't really want to be around people.

With my hair in a messy bun on top of my head, the sun beat down on the back of my neck, making my skin sizzle. I wanted to find somewhere quiet where I could escape the sun. A cluster of trees nestled behind one of the alleys, and I headed in that direction. There was no designated spot to sit, but it didn't matter. Finding a clear spot under the biggest tree, I lay down to rest. The cool grass tickled my exposed skin as I made myself comfortable in the shade.

Closing my eyes, I immediately pictured Callum. As much as it bothered me that he made me feel vulnerable, I could not ignore the attraction. He was sexy as hell. And that voice. I could get lost in it. I recalled my dream from the night before, hoping I could start where I left off.

"I am not impressed with your display of disrespect, Fiona." His eyebrow quirked in question. Wait, 'no. That's not what he was supposed to say. That's not what he was supposed to do!

"I know you are not asleep."

With a gasp, I opened my eyes and shot to a sitting position to see him floating above me, just as fascinating as my subconscious remembered. I couldn't let him know what he did to me. It was too dangerous.

"Where the fuck did you come from?"

"I do not prefer the vulgar words you are throwing around."

"Well I 'do not prefer' you sneaking up on me." I mimicked his speech. "How did you find me, anyway?" I flopped back into the grass and threw an arm over my eyes, trying to appear unaffected. All the while, my body screamed for his touch.

"You summoned me."

"I did not." I rolled over and faced away from him. *Please go away,* I chanted to myself.

"You most certainly did. That is the only reason I would appear at your side."

Ignoring him wasn't working, so I got up and stood at

my full height to try to look him in the eye. "Leave me the fuck alone."

"Have I done something to deserve your rudeness?" While his words were polite, his expression was hard and grim. His arms crossed tightly over his chest, making his muscles appear more prominent than they had been before.

Holding my ground, I took a step toward him, "Have I done something to deserve living in this hell hole? I just wish every fucking body would treat me the way I deserve to be treated!" My rant escalated to a scream before I was finished.

Callum grinned. Widely. One of those cat-that-ate-the-canary types of grins. "Your wish is my command."

Before I knew it, the palms of my hands were pinned to the trunk of the nearest tree, and I bent forward at the waist, making it impossible to straighten myself. Trying to move the lower part of my body proved fruitless because even my feet were stuck, planted to the ground. "What the fuck? Let me go! What are you doing?"

His arms still crossed, he moved into my field of vision. "You have made a wish to be treated in the manner in which you deserve. You, young lady, have displayed atrocious behavior since the moment we met. Therefore, I am going to grant your wish and give you exactly what you deserve."

"W-what exactly do you think I deserve?" His scolding had me feeling like a naughty little girl, and even though I didn't appreciate being spoken to like that, and my current position was not very comfortable, his dominance made my pussy spasm and my panties dampen with need for him..

"You deserve to be spanked soundly." He passed sentence, and I panicked.

"What?" I screeched. "Are you fucking kidding me? You can't spank me! I am a grown woman!"

"As I stated yesterday, you appear grown, but your behavior is that of a spoiled child. Your language does not befit a young woman, and you are treating all you encounter with undeserved disdain. All of these things are unacceptable behavior and, after your backside has been thoroughly chastised, you will apologize to me and to Mary, and you will complete the tasks required of you."

Before I could give him a piece of my mind, a resounding smack landed on my legging-covered bottom. "Ow, you mother fucker! Don't you dare lay another finger on me!" I screamed. He didn't bother answering. His hand rose and fell over and over, and even though I screamed at the top of my lungs for help, no one came to my rescue. My bottom stung, and my arms shook with fatigue. "Please, stop. I'm going to fall!" I begged.

Miraculously, the smacks stopped, and his hands came to my waist, taking the pressure off my arms. Sighing in relief, I attempted to stand on my own, but remained stuck. "Okay, you can let me go, now. I get it. I have been a bitch. I will apologize and do the work."

"Oh, I believe you will. However, we are not finished as of yet."

His hands disappeared, replaced with some sort of a bench with a padded cushion on the top, my hands, and feet still firmly held in place.

"Callum. Let. Me. Go." I ground out the words through clenched teeth. Then the unspeakable happened. My pants fell off—not all the way off, but over my hips and down my backside, coming to rest on my upper thighs. To further complicate the issue, my thong jerked upward, creating a wedgie of fabric between my exposed cheeks. Squeaking with embarrassment, I fought hard to get away, but I couldn't budge. I screamed at the top of my lungs, calling him every name in the book, but he didn't respond.

The spanking got worse,, the sting of his hand amplified by the skin-on-skin contact it hurt more than I could ever have imagined. Without my pants to protect me, he couldn't miss the way my body reacted. I didn't like the pain, but my panties were sopping. My screams died down to pitiful whimpers as I pleaded with him to stop, but I didn't really want him to. The way he had me pinned, the skin of his hand bouncing off my vulnerable flesh, pushed me into a haze of sexual need. The pain spread with each hard smack, and my clit throbbed. I tried to rub my legs together, so primed that any extra pressure would allow me to come, but my position didn't allow for much movement.

"You are a naughty girl. You are not supposed to enjoy your punishment"," Callum stated, yanking my pants down farther and spanking my upper thighs. The change in pain level pulled me out of my lusty fog, and I collapsed against the bench.

My cries of pain turned to sobs, and still he continued. I couldn't keep track of how many times he spanked, the pain in my ass and thighs deep and unrelenting. My skin ached and burned from the top of my ass to the middle of my thighs, so intense I could not tell he had stopped until he tenderly lifted my chin with his index finger. A handkerchief materialized, and he took his time cleaning the tears from my face. I sniffled and hiccupped, but managed staunch the flow of tears.

"C-Can you let m-me g-go now, p-please?" I remained in the uncomfortable position, backside still exposed.

A soft smile touched his features. "Can you tell me why I was forced to punish you so thoroughly?"

I hung my head and squeezed my eyes shut. His question did weird things to my stomach and distracted me from the answer. I shook my head, hoping he would drop the subject. I should have known better.

"If you do not know, perhaps I did not do my job correctly. Perhaps I did not make the impression you wished for?"

My head shot up, and I shook it vehemently. "I didn't wish for this!"

"Oh, little sprite. To quote your own words, 'I just wish every fucking body would treat me the way I deserve to be treated!' I warned you your behavior was unpleasant, but you continued on. Therefore, you got exactly what you deserved." Hearing the words played back in his deep voice made me utterly miserable and for the first time in my entire life, my behavior embarrassed me. My face burned, and I wished I could hide from his intense glare, but I was mesmerized.

"Unfortunately, your wish will only last until your third wish has been granted and I am returned to my chambers. I am aware you asked for 'every fucking body' to treat you how you deserve, but it is against genie rules to control the behavior of another being. Therefore, for the remainder of our time together, it will be my sole responsibility to treat you in a manner befitting your behavior."

I couldn't believe what he said. This wasn't a one-time thing? He planned to do it again? I had now wasted two perfectly good wishes, been subjected to humiliation by the sexiest being I had ever encountered, and it wasn't over. I wanted to make my third wish right then and there, but I didn't want to throw it away to avoid another spanking. I made a mental note to choose my words wisely so as not to screw up again.

"Do not look so grim, little sprite. My reacting to your behavior could also be a positive thing. Rewards will be given as well as punishments."

"What kind of rewards?" At this point I had almost forgotten I was sans pants in public. The pain in my bottom, the burning need in my pussy, and his promises took up all of the mental capacity I had at the moment.

"Good girls receive rewards that make them happy. I cannot tell you what they will be because I do not know. You have given me permission to reward you with the desires of your heart. Only you know what those are. I will be just as surprised as you are when your behavior calls for a reward."

Nodding, I again tried to stand. "Can you please let me go now? This is really embarrassing, and I could get arrested for being exposed in public like this."

Callum chuckled, "Oh, ye of little faith. No one can see or hear us, I have made sure of it. As far as letting you go, I have asked you a question, and you have not yet replied."

Sighing, I went back over the conversation to figure out what he meant. When my brain settled on the information, my mortification renewed. "You punished me because I deserved it."

My pants rose and I was released immediately, swept up into a cradled position in his arms, and all of a sudden, we were in my room. He held tightly, and I snuggled closer. I couldn't remember the last time I had been held like this. My father didn't hug or kiss or even give words of love or praise. Thoughts of him renewed my tears.

"Shh, little sprite. All will be well. You need to rest quietly and regain composure, and then I believe there are a few directives I have given you."

Even though he had returned to being bossy, I was thankful to stop thinking about my father. He didn't deserve my tears. Nodding into his chest, I closed my eyes and listened to the beat of his heart, fascinated how he was not that much different than a real human. Besides the lack of anything below his waist, his goofy speech patterns, and his magic, he was all man. I wiggled in his arms, feeling the pain in my bottom.

"I need to use the restroom"," I whispered.

He set me down, and I righted my clothes.

"Before I leave you to your work, is there something you would like to say to me?"

Knowing exactly what he wanted to hear, I lowered my eyes and nodded. "I'm sorry for my behavior and my language. I will be nicer, I promise."

"And if you do not?"

"I will be punished again?" I guessed with a gulp.

He smiled, "Thank you. That is correct. You are a good girl, and as much as I enjoyed seeing your little bottom wiggle under my hand. I would much rather bring you pleasure than pain. I will return to my chambers, now. You know what to do if you need me."

With that, he was gone.

Chapter Five

The word “‘’pleasure” played over and over in my mind as I cleaned up. My ass was on fire, yet my body wept with need. Eyeing the shower, I decided I was not going to be able to work in this much agony. When the water warmed under my hand I squealed in delight. The plumber had been here, it appeared. I could have wept with relief. That is if I had any more tears left in me—after this afternoon’s events I did not. Stripping quickly, I took a moment to check out my bottom in the mirror. Really, really red. Some areas were darker than others, and bruises formed in a few places. Running my hand over it gently—I gasped in surprise. It was hot to the touch. Turning to face the mirror, I took stock of the rest of my body. My eyes were glazed, my nipples hard peaks, and a cursory swipe of my pussy reminded me of my imminent need.

Hopping into the shower, I took a moment to let the hot water seep into my bones and aching muscles. I took the removable showerhead from its perched position and set the stream to pulse. Directing the water, I used it to tease my entire body, imagining it was Callum’s touch. I started by letting the water massage my nipples, enjoying the slight jolt of pain that turned quickly into pleasure. Moving the stream downward, I widened my stance and positioned the pulsing stream in the perfect place to tease my entire core. With one hand tweaking my nipples and the water teasing my clit, I exploded into a brilliant spiral of overwhelming bliss, barely containing my scream of ecstasy.

My body twitched with tiny aftershocks as I replaced the showerhead and moved back under the stream of hot water. Still set to pulsing, the water pounded the back of my neck and shoulders like a soothing massage. My entire body relaxed, yet my heart felt heavy. Thinking of Callum, I remembered the entire reason behind his harsh punishment. I had treated Mary horribly and needed to apologize right away.

Fortifying myself for what could happen, I went in search of my aunt. It didn't take long to find her. Dressed in baggy pants, and a tank top with the ever-present colorful scarf wrapped around her head, she crouched down, washing the wall underneath one of the sets of shelves. Not for the first time, I wondered how the place got so dirty. Mary was determined, vigilant, and disciplined. It seemed odd she would allow her store to go unkempt for so long.

"Aunt Mary?"

Mary turned to face me, eyes swollen. It appeared as if she had been crying. I closed my eyes and took a deep breath hoping I had not been the cause. "I, um, I'm not very good at this, but I'm, um, sorry. I haven't been the best guest or the most help and… I don't know, this is just really hard for me, but none of that is your fault, and I should control my temper better.

Mary didn't say a word as she set down her wet sponge, removed her rubber gloves, dried her hands, and stood up. The silence was uncomfortable. Everything about this was uncomfortable. Putting my hands behind my back, I brushed my sore backside now covered in a flowy green skirt sans panties. I had attempted more "work friendly" attire, but the fabric rubbed too much against the tender flesh.

Still silent, Mary approached and pulled me into a hug. The first time the woman had touched me since I had arrived and it felt… right. I put my arms around her and pulled tighter, tears filling my eyes. Growing up with no mom and a distant father, I had learned early on physical affection was not to be expected. As I got older, my need for it had dissipated, or had it? I had now been hugged twice in one day, and both times my emotions went haywire.

"I forgive you sweetie. I know that was hard for you. You are just like him." Mary spoke close to my ear.

"Just like who?"

"Your father. He never apologized for anything in all the years I knew him."

I laughed at the idea of Vincent Burelli asking anyone for forgiveness. He would never humble himself. Then again, my friends back home might say the same thing about me. I had been in this town for the better part of two days and already hardly recognized myself.

Mary pulled away first, holding me at arm's length. "I'm proud of you."

That was it. There was nothing left to keep the tears at bay. Mary tightened her grip on my upper arms and would not let go.

"When was the last time someone told you that?" she inquired.

Tears fell freely then, and my brain felt jumbled as I tried to form a response. I could muster only a head shake and a shrug.

"Oh, baby girl, I am so sorry."

"What are you sorry for?" I sniffled.

"I should have never let that man raise you alone."

"That man? He is my father."

Mary's eyes welled with tears, her chin quivered. Her gaze ricocheted back and forth between me and a spot on the floor. "And I am your mother."

I stumbled back and fell onto the antique chest behind me with a hard thud. "You can't be my mother. My mother died when I was two months old."

Mary sighed. "You were two months and seven days old when he took you. I have regretted that day ever since. I told myself his money would keep you safe, but as you grew, I knew I had been wrong. I begged for him to let me see you, spend time with you."

I stood with balled fists to keep from punching the woman. "What the fuck are you talking about? You better stop lying about my mother! She was beautiful, and she sang to me. I have proof."

"Vincent told you that. You have no proof."

"I have heard it with my own ears!" How could this crazy person be the woman my father had waxed poetically about? "You. Are. His. Sister! Either something sick was going on back then or you are a lying bitch!"

"Fiona, I understand you are upset and confused. Please, let me tell you the story."

"I'm done listening! I'm calling my father, and I am going home." I ran from the room before she could spout more lies. I raced out the door and into the street, but then I stopped short. Tears blinded me, and I didn't know the area well enough to know where to go. I had no money, no job, no education besides an unearned high school diploma, and, now, no family.

Sitting on the curb I rested my forearms on my knees, laid my head down, and cried for what felt like the millionth time that day. Everything was so frustrating, and now I was confused about who my parents even were. On one hand, my father, who had raised me, had gotten out of jail the day after his arrest, and hadn't even called me. On the other hand, this pushy, hard headed woman claimed to be my mother. Why tell me now? I was about to be twenty three, a legal adult, and would ultimately be financially set. I didn't need parents. I didn't need anyone. Except, maybe, Callum.

Great, turning to a genie for comfort. A genie who planned to spank me whenever he deemed my behavior unacceptable, apparently. Groaning at the reminder, I pressed my bottom against the edge of the curb to absorb some comfort from the pain. In less than two days, I had gone from wealthy, untouchable heiress to this poor, sad, lonely, pathetically dirty pauper subject to spankings from a mythical creature. I didn't want to waste my last wish, but how much longer could I stand being subjected to his rough handling or stay in this hellhole with a crazy liar?

A warm hand wrapped around my bare shoulder, and I looked up to find the man who consumed my deepest thoughts. "What's wrong, little sprite?"

"Don't call me that!" I tugged my shoulder out of his grasp and scrambled to my feet. I felt too vulnerable sitting while he hovered over me. "I just… I apologized, and then she threw some stupid lie about being my mother at me, if you must know. Has my whole life been a lie? How do I know who's lying? How can I trust anyone after this? How?"

"Take a breath, please."

"You take a breath! I am in a fucking shit storm, and a breath is not going to help me."

"A breath will not solve your problems, no. But it may save you from another paddling. That is one for the vulgar phrase. If I get to the count of three, I will be forced to discipline you, and I will make sure you do not like any of it."

I immediately lost my bravado and fell into his arms. The day had been full of twists and turns, and it all seemed too much to handle.

His spicy scent filled my nostrils, and I burrowed as close as I could, barely noticing he had moved us to the privacy of my room. Lifting me into his arms, he settled us both on my bed. I allowed him to take care of me, thankful I didn't have to think anymore.

"Now, would you like to speak calmly about the information you received from your aunt?"

"She says she's my mother, but my mother is dead. My father told me about her. Why would he lie to me? She has to be lying." My words came fast as my heart pounded again.

"Shhh. Take a breath, little sprite. Breathe with me."

I nodded and lay back down on his chest trying to mimic his breathing pattern. It helped me regain composure instead of spiraling into a panic attack. It would be nice to have him around if he could help me calm down like this. With everything going on I was becoming more and more anxious as the days passed. The only time I didn't feel like everything crumbled beneath my feet was when I was with him. He froze time and knew how to control my outbursts. If anyone back home heard I allowed a man to hold me like this, they would never believe it. I was independent and stone cold. No one took the time to pick through the ice surrounding my heart. This man, though, this man didn't have to pick. The first time he touched me, the walls melted away. What was it about him?

"Good girl, now let's try once more to complete our conversation in a calm and polite manner, shall we?"

"Yeah, whatever. We can try." Annoyed, I didn't want to talk. I just wanted to be left alone. Okay, a lie. I did not want him to leave, but I would love it if he would shut up.

"Sprite, you need to learn to show respect. 'Yeah, whatever' is not an appropriate response, especially to someone who is trying to assist you and has the ability to display his displeasure through a sound spanking."

I pulled my shoulders up to my ears and gulped.

"From this point forward, you will respond to me at all times with a 'Yes, Sir' or a 'No, Sir.' Once your manners improve, we may discuss times where such formality is unnecessary."

I shot up so I could see his face. He had to be joking. "Sir? You think I am going to walk around calling you Sir?"

"You will, or you will be punished."

Jumping off my bed, I turned on him. "Look, You may be some all-powerful genie or what-the-fuck-ever, but I will be damned if I am going to bow at your feet."

"Two."

"What?" I screeched.

"That is the second time you have used a vulgar phrase. One more, and you will be disciplined. I have not asked you to bow, yet," he said, grinning unapologetically.

"Oh my God! You are seriously impossible!"

"And you are seriously in need of another attitude adjustment," he countered. I was fired up, and he was completely unfazed. It was pissing me off to no end.

"Go fuck yourself!" I screamed within a foot of his face.

He shook his head, "Okay, little sprite, that's three." He

raised his hand and snapped his fingers, and I found myself facing a corner in my room.

"Yeah right, dude. Not gonna happen, there is no way I am standing in the corner like a naughty five year old. I tried to turn my body, but my feet wouldn't move. More than that, I was actually floating. "Oh come on, that's not even fair."

"You may not speak during cornertime. You are to stand silently and consider the actions that brought this on. I gave you warnings; you decided not to heed them."

"Heed this," I yelled, flipping him the bird.

Another snap and my arms were pinned to my sides. "Would you like to keep pushing?"

"No, I would like to be let go." I strained to break the hold, but I could barely move. "Put. Me. Down." I growled, clenching my teeth so hard it made my jaw ache.

"I will not. Not until you pay your penance."

"You are an asshole, you know that?"

Another snap and. I couldn't move at all and my mouth would not open. It was like being in a full body straight jacket with my mouth taped shut. I squirmed and fought, but nothing worked. I called him every name in the book in my throat, but he didn't seem to care. Time ticked by, and I got so tired. Staring at the corner bored me, and my body started to ached from trying to escape. It felt as though I had just completed a full body workout.

With a sigh I gave up. Anger and frustration were getting me nowhere, and I wanted to be done. I accepted my fate and stared at the corner, still and silent.

"That's a good girl," he praised as he slowly released me and brought me to stand in front of him. "Now that you have found a calm place, do you anticipate any more outbursts?"

I shook my head. I wasn't planning on anything except going to bed. This day had been utter crap.

"Little sprite, how are you supposed to address me?"

I closed my eyes and took a fortifying breath before forcing out the damn phrase. "No, Sir."

"There now see, it was certainly not worth all that fuss, now was it?"

I counted to ten in my head to keep myself from punching him in the mouth.

"It's late, and you have had a long day. Get ready for bed, and I will tuck you in."

I left my room without a word and went to the bathroom to get ready, more to get away from him than to actually follow orders, sick of him telling me what to do. That wish had been so dumb. How could I screw something up so terribly? Three wishes should have been a gift, but they felt more like a curse. I finished up and dragged myself back to the room. Callum had shut the light off and lit a candle on the dresser. The whole space smelled of lavender. My bed was turned down, and he waited beside it. The entire scene was so sweet and, even though I had been a bitch, again, he was back to taking care of me. As soon as I lay down, he covered me with the blanket and kissed my forehead.

"Sleep well, little sprite."

Chapter Six

"Okay, so I wasted two whole wishes. Can I just use my last wish to—"

"No." Callum interrupted.

"You don't even know what I was going to ask"." I stopped sweeping and threw him my signature glare.

"Do I not?" He folded his arms over his muscled chest, regarding me with that frustrating quirk of his brow. The look did funny things to my insides and made me want to curl in a ball at his feet. It drove me nuts how hard I had to fight my developing feelings, but his ego was big enough. He didn't need to know how he affected me.

"Not unless you can read my mind." I put my hands on my hips and held back from tapping my toe. His Mr. Know-it-all attitude rubbed me the wrong way every time.

"I may be able to hear you when your thoughts call to me, but reading your mind is not one of my skills. However, I have been a genie for six generations, my father for seventeen before me, and his father for twelve before him. They passed their knowledge down, and I have gained much through my own experience. Every single woman we have served has made the same request you were about to make, and the answer has been the same thing each of those times."

"You are a cocky bastard." I turned back to my chore. If he wanted to be a jerk, I would ignore him altogether.

"I do."

I stomped over to the counter and propped the broom against it before turning on him. "Since you know everything, I am going to ask, why don't you enlighten me on all things genie, and I will be a good little student and listen."

"Did you really just roll your fucking eyes at me?" *I know he didn't roll his eyes at me.*

"Did you really speak to me in that manner?" He scooted closer, never being one to back down from one of my tantrums.

I wasn't backing down either. I widened my stance, ready for a fight. "If you can be rude, so can I."

"I have said nothing that could be construed rude. You, however, have expressed attitude in your demeanor, called me a name, and spat a vulgar word in my direction. I believe I have warned you about your mouth, have I not?"

Stand your ground, Fi. He knew goading me pissed me off, and he did it on purpose. Punishment or no punishment, I was going to give him a piece of my mind. "Look, you float around and lord over me with this domineering façade, and when I ask a simple question, you cut me off."

"False wishes can be counted against you, even if they are against code. I attempted to save you from throwing your last one away. I apologize for not explaining myself straightaway. That is still no excuse for your tantrum."

I couldn't keep eye contact as I thought about how strong my reaction had been. At home I was like ice woman. No one could ruffle me, and it bothered me on so many levels when he did. "I'm sorry, too." I conceded.

Callum gave a nod but stayed quiet. He had a way of giving me time to think when I needed it, even if it wasn't what I wanted. The silence made me uncomfortable, and shifted from foot to foot.

"How about we discuss more of the rules and avoid another episode such as this?"

I let go of the breath burning my lungs. “Okay, yeah. Good idea.” He gestured to a chair, and I sat down. “Are there a lot of them? I’m not so great with rules.”

He placed an open palm on his cheek and shook his head. “You don’t say?”

“Ha. Ha.”

“There are not many I believe you need to be aware of, but the few you do are quite important.”

The front door to the shop opened, and Mary came in with an armload of groceries. “Fi, be a dear and help with these, will you?” she puffed, but before I could respond, she screamed and dropped the load she had been carrying. Apples scattered in every direction.

“Callum?” she whispered, white as a ghost.

I jumped to my feet, “You two know each other?” Looking back and forth between the two gave me the answer. His smirk, her stunned expression. Clearly I was missing something. “What is going on around here?”

“It’s been a long time,” Mary whispered, eyes still trained on the man floating in front of me.

“I was once your mother’s genie, as I am yours.” He made it sound like that should be common knowledge. It definitely was not.

“You… you were her genie? When?” Questions flooded my mind, but none would come together as a finished thought.

“She was a little younger than you. Isn’t that correct, Mary?”

“Yes, Sir.”

A smug smile spread across his face. “I see you remember our time together.”

Mary’s hands went behind her, and her face darkened to the shade of a ripe tomato.

"You... you spanked her?" My voice reached decibels that would have made a dog yelp and run for cover.

"Did you think you were the only naughty girl I have granted wishes for? I have been assigned to the women in your family for six generations. And I have been tasked with disciplining them all in order to complete my mission."

I could not believe what I heard. My genie, the man who was breaking down all of my carefully constructed walls, had served and spanked my mother? It would have been easier to accept some past stranger had gotten a few wishes granted, but he knew my mother? I couldn't help but feel betrayed. All this time he knew who she was and hadn't said a word about it. "I... this... you?"

"Take a breath"," Callum instructed.

I did and closed my eyes. Nothing would get answered if I couldn't pose the question. "Can we start from the beginning?"

"Mary, would you mind giving us some privacy? I believe you know this story well." She nodded and hastily gathered the spilled groceries before hiking up the stairs to the apartment.

"What did you do to her? She has not been speechless since I got out of the cab."

"Your mother has always been quite the chatterbox. I instituted the same discipline with her as I have you. She was quite the handful. Her lack of words probably had something to do with seeing me again for the first time in over twenty years."

"I guess so, maybe, but... did you know who I was?"

"Of course I did. We were destined to meet."

I hated that word. "I don't believe in destiny."

"Roll your eyes again and you can listen to this story with your nose pressed to the wall."

"I'm sorry, Sir." Squeezing my eyes shut, I hoped not to find myself floating in that awful position again.

"That's my good girl. Now, would you like to sit down and listen?"

I nodded and fell back down on the chair.

Taking a deep breath, he delved into the story of his past. "I was born approximately two hundred years ago to Olivia and Alastair. My father was a genie before he met my mother, which destined their first born son to follow in his footsteps when he came of age. I was their first born. Growing up knowing what my future held, I was not schooled like normal children but by my father. He taught me what it was going to be like and what I would likely encounter, explained all of the stringent rules and regulations. There are many things genies are not allowed to do and if our rules are broken, the consequence is dire."

Ominous. "How can a genie face consequences?"

"Everyone has consequences, little sprite. I am no different. If a genie should attempt to break one of the rules, he is relegated to his chamber for eternity. Complete and total isolation. It is a horrible fate."

"But don't you spend most of your time there, anyway?"

Callum nodded, "Indeed. However, when I am waiting for my next grantee, I am in a deep slumber. The worlds are separated by time, your day equivalent of my hour. Time passes much faster in your world. It is how we appear to be so much younger than our years would allow. It is also why time passes slower when you are in my presence. It is the universe's attempt to balance the difference."

"Okay, so how come you have been with only my family? I thought genies bounced around to whoever found the magic lamp? Oh my God. Would you listen to me? I'm a psychopath."

"Please refrain from self-degradation." His eyebrow rose, and I slunk down against the back of the chair. "May I continue?"

"Yes, Sir."

"Thank you. Each genie is assigned to a specific family. I knew the bloodline of my first mistress would be that of my future mate. This is the part pertaining to you. We have had some conversations where you have shared your feelings with me. I have refrained from doing so for fear your heart will be broken, but the truth is, I believe you are her."

"I am who?" I sat up straight hoping he meant what I heard. I was falling in love with him. I had been since the first moment he didn't back down from me. I needed his strength in my life. It was scary to think about it. I knew we couldn't have a relationship, so I had felt pretty lost and confused.

"When you need me, I can feel it like an ache in my chest. You call me to you with your thoughts, and I find myself thinking about you often. My father waited seventeen generations for his love. I did not think mine would come so soon. I also fear my mind is flawed. I have not felt fear for over a hundred years."

His eyes carried a pained look, and I wanted to comfort him. I got up and took his hand, hoping to infuse him with whatever strength he may need. "What are you afraid of?"

"Losing you." His eyes bore into my soul. A fist grabbed hold of my heart, squeezing tight enough to burst it at any moment.

"The normal sequence of events would lead me to be returned to my chamber after your third wish is granted. If you are indeed my soul mate, I will be granted my freedom, and we can live out the rest of our days as man and wife."

"And if we are not…"

"Then it is likely you will never see me again."

The fist tightened, and I barely contained my sorrow. "I will never make my third wish. I will keep it forever. Then you can stay with me."

"That's not how it works, my little sprite. If indeed you never make your third wish, then we will be together only in farce. I will never be able to love you the way it is intended for a man to love his woman, and you will never be fulfilled. If your life should come to an end before your third wish is granted, then I have failed in my mission, and I will be punished. There is no way around it, and to try to cheat is to open yourself to very unappealing consequences."

"That's just not fair."

He caught my tear on his thumb. "Life is not fair. Have you not learned this in your twenty-three years on this planet?"

"I have learned more about life in the last few days than I ever did at home with my father. Mary is… different. She pushes me and has a way of making me feel good about myself and what I'm doing. She frustrates the sh… crap out of me. I just can't trust her."

"Your mother is a good woman who made very bad mistakes, but you need to find forgiveness in your heart for her. She loves you."

Needing to feel his strength, I leaned in for a hug. "I don't know how."

His arms folded around me, and he laid a kiss to the crown of my head. "It will come."

That small comfort offered exactly what I needed, and my pounding, aching heart slowed to match the cadence of

Callum's. "Can you tell me the rest of the rules? I don't want to mess up and get you in trouble. I don't want you to punished on my account."

He stroked my hair. "Yes, I will. You need to be aware nothing you do can directly cause me to be punished, unless you put yourself in danger and lose your life. This is why I am so hard on you. You need to keep yourself safe and allow me to guide you."

"My potty mouth isn't going to kill me."

He chuckled. "You are correct. However, I do not like it."

"I know, I know. Back to the rules."

With my ear pressed against his chest I could feel the words spoken.

"Genies are very powerful beings, and that could be dangerous to the future of the human race. We were given rules to keep that from happening."

"How can one genie endanger the entire world?"

"I can end your life with the snap of my fingers."

A nervous laugh bubbled out of me. I had never thought about it before, but now that he brought it up, it was a little freaky. "Oh. Well okay then."

"If I were to do that, you would be dead, and I would be punished, instantly."

"Is there like a genie council or something watching you all?"

He shook his head. "No, nothing like that. It is hard to explain. It is the universe that does not allow it."

"That makes no sense. How does the universe control you?" There was a reason I didn't believe in all the magical crap. I had questions, and the answers made no sense.

"Let me try to explain. Thousands of years ago, when the first genie found his mate, they bore twin boys. The older of the two was, of course, destined to become a genie, however the younger boy was jealous of all the attention his brother received. They hated one another with a deep passion, and the day the older son was granted his powers, he used them against his brother, ultimately ending his life."

"That's awful."

"Indeed. Their father's distress overwhelmed him, and he spent his entire life seeking out a way to stop his eldest son. His mission kept him alive for hundreds of years, long enough for him to contrive a spell and see the birth of his grandson. He stole the baby and used the small amount of power he had left to place a spell over the child, taking away any more chances that a genie should be allowed to harm another without consequence. He died shortly afterward, but his spell worked and is now built into all of us."

"It's still crazy to me you even exist. There's no such thing as magic. You are a myth, a storybook character." I don't know if I was trying to convince him or me at that point.

He quirked a brow. "I don't believe storybook characters have the capability of paddling your backside."

The veiled threat made me giggle. "I don't *deserve* a spanking, so you can't give me one."

"Oh, little sprite. You have much to learn. You always deserve one. Don't you know, good girls get spankings, too?"

I caught the glint in his deep purple eyes. The spanking had definitely excited me, but I would never admit it. It was too embarrassing. His unyielding power, coupled with the feeling of helplessness and his hand so close to my sex had made me crazy with arousal. Even now, the memory of the experience made me wet.

"I see you like the idea. Your little pussy wept for me

when I bound you to the tree. You cannot hide from Daddy in that position."

Groaning, I buried my face in his chest to hide the blush and escape his knowing gaze. It didn't matter what position he had me in, I couldn't hide things from him. Especially the feelings he evoked in me. My body had such a visceral reaction to him, I didn't stand a chance.

He placed a finger underneath my chin and forced me to look at him. "The truth. Would you like to know what it is like to get a good girl spanking?"

I bit my lip and forced myself not to agree to quickly. I would give anything to feel his power like that again, even take a humiliating spanking. "What's the difference between good girl and bad girl spankings?" I asked.

"Be a good girl, and you will find out," he replied with a wink.

Chapter Seven

After a week of cleaning merchandise off shelves, Mary decided we needed a change of scenery. My arms and shoulders had developed a perpetual ache, so I was all for something different. That is, until I saw the disaster she called "her "files." Receipts, tax documents, employee information, you name it. It had been haphazardly thrown into boxes and shoved in the closet with zero rhyme or reason to any of it. If it had been up to me, I would have thrown all of it in the fire pit, but apparently that wasn't an option.

"I have to say, this kinda surprises me." I was only semi-teasing. As a rule, Mary kept things in order. The shop initially looked like a haphazard mess, but, as time went on, I learned there was an organization to it that she understood. She liked it that way. This was the furthest thing from order and organization I had ever seen.

"Yes, dear. I'm sure that it does. We all have our areas we can improve on. Paperwork and recordkeeping are mine. We just need to go through and figure out what's important and what's not and then organize it from there." She shoved a box in my arms, and I swept my foot on the floor to create a clean spot for my workspace. Sitting down against the wall, I looked up and realized I was directly across from the secret room where I'd found Callum's bottle. With everything that had happened, I had completely forgotten about it and all of its contents. I shivered, remembering how creeped out I had been when I saw all that crap, but then I got that familiar tummy flutter as my thoughts turned to Callum. As usual, I tried to push the thoughts away by focusing on the task at hand. I mean, really, who spent all their time obsessing about a sexy genie? Ugh. The busywork helped, but thoughts of him niggled just below the surface, ever present.

After hours spent sorting paperwork, my butt was numb, my throat dry, and my stomach empty. Time to be done for a bit. I stood up and stepped over my carefully constructed piles to get my water bottle.

"So can you explain that room to me?" I asked hesitantly. The question had been lingering on the tip of my tongue all day, and I could no longer hold it in.

She stood and stretched her back, frowning resignedly. "What would you like to know?"

"Why does it exist? Is that all your stuff?" I posed my questions carefully so as not to come off as judgmental, but the things in that room were weird, and I was concerned I might be living with a crazy person

Mary looked at me with a weary expression and sighed. "Let's go upstairs and have some lunch. We can chat while we eat."

She left quickly as if trying to put some distance between her and the creepy little room. I followed her without a word, becoming more and more worried about her answer.

Upstairs, Mary pulled out all of the fixings for sandwiches as I cleared off the merchandise drying on the table. She still didn't speak.

"If you don't want to talk about it, then we don't have to." I offered.

"I'm fine, dear."

She didn't seem fine, but I didn't feel like arguing, and I

wanted to know the answers. We made our sandwiches and sat at the table with bottles of cold water. God I wanted a Coke.

"Before I met your father, I had an interest in the darker sides of magic," she began out of nowhere. "I dabbled in all sorts of witchcraft for years. When Callum came into my life, he did his darndest to get me out of it, but I was wrapped in deep, obsessed with potions and spells and everything in between. Some of the stuff I did was dangerous. I was always on a wild goose chase for this ingredient or that. Always in search of something."

I listened to the tale, completely weirded out but trying not to judge. "When I met your father, I fell head over heels, and I quit it all, but..." She trailed off, looking around the room, and I could tell this part was difficult. "When I got pregnant, I got scared, and I tried to conjure something to end the pregnancy. You have to understand I was young and addicted to drugs." At this point in the story, she avoided making eye contact with me. Abortion? Was she serious? Taking a deep breath I schooled my features. I was angry but wanted to hear the entire story. This was the first time she had opened up to me. "I was thankfully unsuccessful, and when your father found out, he was furious. He locked me away in his house and would not allow me to go anywhere or do anything without his approval and supervision. It was horrible, but I deserved it." She paused, taking a bite of her sandwich. I wanted to scream at her to continue, my stomach in such knots I was not going to be able to eat.

"He forced me to marry him, insisting no Burelli would ever be born a bastard. I tried to love him. I wanted to appreciate the care I received. I was clean and sober for the first time since I was a teenager. But I hated him. I knew deep down he was not a good man and we would not have a happy future together. I stayed for you." She finally looked at me again, with sad and haunted eyes. I struggled with what I should say or do. I already knew how this story ended. Maybe I should have asked her to stop, but it was like watching a train wreck. I knew the train was going to crash, but I couldn't take my eyes away.

"In the end, I wasn't strong enough. I went back to the drugs and… he took you away. He told me if I ever came for you he would kill us both and be done with the whole thing. I couldn't let him hurt you, so I did as told. I took his hush money, got clean for the final time, and bought this place. I put all of my things in that room and have not touched them since."

"Wait, he threatened to kill me?" I was stuck on one haunting sentence. It seemed hard to believe. He was a crap father, but he had always made sure I was taken care of.

"If he had only threatened me, I would have taken the risk."

With a sinking stomach, I realized Mary had no real reason to lie to me.

I hadn't spoken to my father since his arrest, and I had no plans to remedy the situation. Once I had my money, I would be gone for good and never look back. I had already made that decision, but the new information sealed the deal. I was simply a responsibility, but why? Because I was a Burelli? What a bunch of horse shit!

"Talk to me dear." Mary reached out and took my hand. "I see you struggling. I will answer any questions you have. You deserve the whole truth."

"Why did my father let me see you once? Why didn't we ever get to come back?"

"I pleaded with him to let me visit with you. We had so

much fun, do you remember?" Her smile warmed my heart, but I didn't remember much.

"You hugged me a lot." It was the one thing that stuck out. Physical affection was not something my father offered me, so being around someone who gave hugs freely had made a huge impact.

Her smile widened, and some of the pain faded from her face. As much as that story sucked, and I wanted to be mad, this woman had been through hell, and the bottom line was, she took me in when no one else would. If my remembering her hugs gave her some light, then so be it.

Chapter Eight

My alarm squealed, and I jumped out of bed. "It's my birthday." I quietly celebrated. In the past, I would wake up to an empty house. There would usually be a card on the kitchen counter from my father, but never even signed by him. I would happily take the cash out of it, dump the card in the trash, and head to the spa for a full day of pampering. The end of the day would consist of clubbing with my friends, getting shitfaced, and hooking up with the first guy I deemed fit. It felt good in the moment, but the following days were filled with loneliness, frustration, and self-loathing.

Today, I was going to put on some ragged clothes, eat a bowl of cereal with whole milk, and spend the day scrubbing antiques as I had for the past few weeks. My nails were all chipped to hell, I could feel calluses forming on my hands, and my hair was a dry ratty wreck, but I couldn't be bothered with that stuff anymore. I didn't care. Okay, so maybe I cared a little bit, but definitely not as much. My life now had a sense of purpose. Spending time working in the shop with Mary had made me realize how empty and shallow all of my past relationships were. The fact that she was my mother was still a bit unbelievable, and we had not talked about it since the day I found out, but I was totally okay with that. She showed me a huge amount of respect by letting me to come to her when I was ready. There also had been no talk about me moving out when the money came through. It was the elephant in the room. I hadn't even talked about it with Callum, who had become my confidante, best friend, and deepest fantasy.

He made subtle comments about using my third wish on my birthday, but there were two problems with that. One, I didn't want the things I used to want anymore. Life was less about money and power and more about love and purpose. And, two, I didn't know what would happen to him. My relationship with him was an exciting adventure I didn't want to end. He was unlike any other person I had ever met. He had all of the characteristics I had ever hoped for in a man, even though he wasn't even human. A life without Callum was the last thing I wanted to imagine. Never knowing what real love felt like, my feelings toward him confused and scared me, but they also excited and filled me with hope.

The smell of coffee permeated the air, and I thought I might be dreaming, but it was so real. I could taste the sweet fumes! I whipped open the curtain and gasped at what I saw. Front and center in the middle of the kitchen counter stood a shiny new coffeemaker.

"Cream or sugar?" Mary asked as she pulled the cup out from under the machine and placed it in front of her.

I squealed in delight and ran to the kitchen, almost tackling her to the floor in a bear hug. "You got me coffee? Best birthday present ever!" I exclaimed. "No cream, no sugar, just gimme!" Letting go of her, I picked up the steaming mug and held it to my nose. Wasting no time, I took the first sip and just about died and went to heaven. "Oh my God. It's been so long."

"It's only been a few weeks." Mary teased.

"That's forever in coffee years!" I filled with contentment as the coffee warmed my stomach. "Thank you. This is the most thoughtful gift anyone has ever given me," I confessed, unable to make eye contact.

She reached out and grabbed my hand, "You deserve this and so much more. You have worked so hard around here. I don't know how to thank you for staying. I figured…" Her voice began to shake. "I figure you can take this wherever you decide to go, and maybe remember your time here."

I set the cup down and pulled her into another hug. I didn't know what to say, the words caught in my throat. I could leave now. The money would hit my account, and I would be free. I could go anywhere I wanted, make a life for myself, but it sounded so… lonely.

Mary pulled away, wiping her eyes with the corner of her kimono, "I'm sorry to get emotional, dearie. I never thought I would get to spend a birthday with you, and I'm just so thankful."

I smiled as my own eyes filled with tears. I'd never thought I would spend a birthday with my mom either.

"Is this how we are to spend the day?" Callum's voice sounded before he materialized.

"You are so rude! Can't you see we're having a moment?" I joked.

Quirking his eyebrow, he crossed his arms over his chest and waited. Rolling my eyes, I approached him and adopted a very unrepentant stance. "I'm sorry for my petulance, Sir. Please forgive me?"

I peeked up to see him smiling and jumped into his arms. Nuzzling my neck, he gave a sharp bite. "You will pay for that later, you know?"

I blushed, remembering his birthday promise. "I'm counting on it."

His chuckle rumbled through his chest and, with my

legs wrapped around him, I felt it directly in my pussy. "My little sprite, you are full of yourself this morning."

"I had coffee! Look!" Grabbing his hand I dragged him in front of the machine. Doing my best Vanna White impression, I explained its importance, "You see, Sir? This little piece of machinery has the power to make lifesaving cups of pure delight. With a single push of this button"—I pointed to the lit blue circle—"an elixir will magically pour from the spout, filling the waiting cup that should then be delivered to the waiting hands of me, preferably before my feet have even touched the floor." I placed my hands on my hips. "I'm gonna need you to learn how to use this thing because you are now my official delivery boy."

Callum mimicked my stance and my facial expression. "I'm gonna need to teach you a lesson if you think you can talk to me like that."

His sudden seriousness shocked the hell out of me. "But it's my birthday!"

"Oh, I know what day it is."

"I'm supposed to be the queen on my birthday." I pouted.

Lifting my chin with his finger, he winked. "You are always my princess, but I am the king, and that is the way it will always be."

"Do I at least get a crown?" I summoned the most pitiful look I could muster.

Callum snapped his fingers, and a stunning tiara appeared in his hand. The stones sparkled, their reflections sending shiny little dots all over the room. My heart filled with excitement, but I did my best to hide it with a bored sigh. "I guess that will do."

As he placed the fragile jewelry atop my head, he smiled and rolled his eyes "You, little girl, are in for one hell of a wakeup call tonight. I hope you aren't planning on sitting tomorrow," he growled for only me to hear.

I giggled, excited for what was to come. My good girl spankings had been amazing, but he had talked up this birthday spanking so much my body shook with anticipation. Getting up onto my toes, I strained for a kiss. Callum obliged with a chaste peck but pulled back before I could get more. "Happy Birthday, sweetheart."

"Thank you, Daddy."

A sniffle broke our reverie, and we turned to see my mother sobbing.

"What's wrong?" I asked as concern slammed into me.

"N-nothing, dear. Absolutely nothing. Everything is perfect."

Callum crossed his arms and squinted his eyes slightly. "You are lying."

Both of us gasped at his accusation, and I swiveled my head back and forth between the two, unsure what to say or do.

"Please, Callum. Not today," she begged. "Tomorrow, maybe, but just not today."

Eyeing her shrewdly, he nodded. "Tomorrow, then."

"Wait, what? What just happened here?" Frustration grew in my chest.

"Fi, look at me, dearie." Mary called. "Please, let me have this day with you. Let's celebrate and enjoy each other's company. I have a whole host of things planned, and I don't want anything to get in the way. Please."

I sighed, I was worried, but, truthfully, I had been looking forward to spending my special day with the two people I loved. A sigh of resignation and a nod of my head gave them permission to proceed with our celebration.

"Okay, first things first. Callum, you can have breakfast

with us, but then I don't want to see you again until dinner."

Callum nodded. "I know the plan. You get her for the day, but the night belongs to me. I am making you both dinner."

Mary and I laughed, but I spoke up. "Are you going to snap something together?" I mimicked his magical snapping motion.

"As a matter of fact, little sprite, I happen to be an excellent cook."

"I'll believe it when I see it."

"And see it you shall." We stared intensely at each other, breaking into grins at exactly the same time. It was going to be such a fun day, and night.

With orders from Mary, I finished my cup of coffee and headed into the bathroom to shower while she made breakfast and chatted away with Callum. I waited for the jealousy to set in, like it did when I saw them interact so comfortably, but nothing came. Instead my heart rejoiced that the two people who meant the most in the world to me cared for each other also. I stripped off my clothes and hopped under the warm spray. Normally, I took the time to enjoy the shower, letting the water penetrate my sore muscles and allowing fantasies of Callum to run wild, but, today, I didn't want to waste any time. I rushed through everything and got dressed just in time to see the table being set with a breakfast feast.

"Wow, how did you do this so fast?" I asked as my chair scooted away from the table, inviting me to sit.

I eyed Callum across the room, and he winked. He had admitted using his magic to pamper me when I "deserved" it was one of his favorite things to do. Pulling out chairs, opening doors, all of the gentlemanly gestures done with a snap of his fingers. “You’re lazy,” I teased as I took my seat.

“And you’re a brat,” he countered, taking his usual seat next to me.

Mary sat on his left, giving it the feel that Callum sat at the head of the table, even though it was only big enough to seat four. “I whipped it all up, and your boyfriend helpfully sped up the cook time. We make a good team.” She grinned.

I shook my head as I watched my man dish up my breakfast of homemade quiche, bacon, and a big glass of orange juice. “This looks amazing.” I forked a big bite, making sure to get the crust and filling of the quiche. The egg, spinach, and cheese blended together perfectly, each ingredient enhancing the taste of the others, and the flaky crust melted on my tongue. The bacon crumbled when I picked it up, telling me it was cooked to my liking. “You two have outdone yourselves. Seriously, this is the best breakfast I have ever had, and I’ve been to the best restaurants all over the world. Sorry, babe. No way are you going to outdo this meal with your dinner.”

“Challenge accepted,” he teased, in between bites. It still amazed me he was so fully human, yet, he wasn’t. He inhaled the meal, finishing before I was even halfway done. “What do you ladies have planned for the day?” he asked leaning back in his seat, a look of utter satisfaction on his face.

Mary had refused to tell me anything, and she blatantly ignored Callum’s question in favor of another bite, obviously still not ready to give away the information.

He shook his head and smirked in her direction. “You should consider yourself lucky I can’t deal with your insolence anymore.”

I cringed. Even though my jealousy had quelled, kinds

of comments set me back. I swallowed hard and pushed past it. No fighting on my birthday. I would talk to him about it another day. He must have felt my reaction, somehow, because he reached under the table and squeezed my knee in comfort. I chose to ignore it and took another piece of bacon. Mary stayed eerily quiet, further raising my anxiety that something was wrong, but again I shook it out and focused on the day ahead. I knew that was what she wanted me to do

We finished our food and began our cleanup ritual.

"Hey, ladies," Callum called. He made a show of raising his right hand in the air and putting his thumb and middle finger together. I smiled, knowing what was coming, and, as his fingers clicked, the entire mess disappeared.

"Where have you been for two weeks while we have been busting our asses cleaning around this place?" I exclaimed before slapping both of my hands over my mouth.

Callum clicked his tongue in disapproval.

I shook my head as hard as I could. "Please don't. It's my birthday," I whined.

Rubbing his fingers together, he contemplated before I heard the snap. My feet lifted off the floor, and I was turned into the corner, my ability to move or speak completely taken away. I hated time out, and he knew it. "Birthday or not, vulgar words are never necessary, and the fact we are still dealing with this daily makes it apparent I need to be more serious."

I whimpered and stared at the wall in front of me.

He passed sentence. "You will stay there until your mother is ready to leave." He spoke to Mary next. "Take your time. Our girl needs a reminder about proper language."

Being unable to turn or speak was the most frustrating thing. I could move only my eyes, and that got me nothing. I growled in the back of my throat when I heard the shower turn on. *Of course, of course. She is going to take a shower. Didn't she shower last night?* There was no noise behind me, so I had no idea where Callum was or what he was doing. *Happy Birthday to me. Happy Birthday to me. I hate the corner. Happy birthday to me.* I sang in my head, not realizing I was humming until a sharp line of pain slashed across my bottom. My eyes widened, and I whined before falling silent. I hated that kind of spank. The sting was unbearable, and it left a welt, and the pain spread from there. I would feel it for the entire day, which I knew was his plan. He loved to keep me aware of him. Even when we weren't together, he could tell when I was thinking about him. It was equally frustrating and arousing. If only he would put out the fires he so loved to start. *Tonight, please let it be tonight.*

While I was lost in thought, the time seemed to move a little faster, and before I knew it Mary saying she was ready to go. I held my breath until I heard the telltale snap that would bring me face to face with my disciplinarian. I let out the breath and shook out my muscles as I was lowered in front of him. He waited expectantly for me to speak, and not daring to push my luck, I spat out my apology. "I'm sorry for using vulgar language. I am smart enough to think of better ways to say things, and it is disrespectful to you and myself when I choose not to."

Callum smiled proudly. "Good girl. Now, go have a nice day with your mother." He leaned in for a kiss and, before he could pull away I wrapped my arms around his neck and jumped into his arms. He growled into my mouth, deepening the kiss for a minute before untangling my hands from the back of his head. "Behave yourself."

"Yes, Sir," I said in a singsong tone as I joined Mary at the door.

To my delight, our first stop for the morning was the salon. We drove out of our little town and into the neighboring city. Since Mary had spent the better part of two weeks teasing me about my soft hands and feet and rolling her eyes whenever I whined about chipping a nail, this was almost a bigger surprise than the coffeemaker. Once again I was overwhelmed with the amount of thought and effort she had put into making this day special. Sitting in the massage chair with my feet in the hot water, I looked over at my mother. Her head was back, her eyes closed, giving her a very relaxed look. I liked seeing peace on her face. The last two weeks had been hard on us. We were tired, but the shop was coming along, and seeing the progress was fulfilling. Not for the first time, I thought about how different my life would have been had I been raised by my mother. Mother. That feeling was becoming less and less foreign, and there had been a couple occasions when I had almost called her Mom. For some reason, I just hadn't let it come.

Reaching over, I took her hand. She opened her eyes, and we exchanged contented looks. "Thank you."

Her eyes filled with tears, and she nodded.

"For everything." I finished.

"The pleasure has been all mine, my dear."

"Are you, okay? You've been so quiet and teary."

"Today is about you. Where would you like to go for lunch?"

I wanted to pry, but the stubborn woman would not crack if she didn't want to, and pushing would just lead to frustrations. Choosing wisdom, I addressed the question. "Is there any good sushi nearby?"

A smile spread across her face. "Girl after my own heart. I haven't had sushi in years, but it's my favorite. I'm sure we can find a place."

I pulled out my phone and searched the Internet. We read reviews about some local places and settled on one that looked promising, conveniently located in a mall. It amazed me how comfortable she was being pampered. Her attitude about all things worldly had led me to assume she was a small town hermit who would be uncomfortable around the finer things in life. Contrary to that belief, she acted as if she did things like this every day. It made the entire outing a heck of a lot more fun.

After being pampered, we tried on clothes at the mall and chattered like old girlfriends. While we had carried on hours and hours of conversation working in the shop, this was different. This was the first time I truly felt like we were family instead of strangers trying to make it work. We went into every store, finding objects of interest and things to laugh and joke about. When we got to the sushi place, we both collapsed in our seats.

"I forgot what hard work shopping can be," Mary announced with a soft laugh.

I shook my head, "You would think this would be easy with the long hours we have been putting in at the store."

"For you, maybe," Mary teased. "I'm an old lady."

I rolled my eyes. "Oh please. You have me by twenty years, and we all know that you have better stamina than I do."

"It's catching up to me. You will be running circles around me soon."

Not able to decide on what we wanted when the waitress came, we ordered an obscene amount of food. "We are never going to eat all that," I joked.

"Did you forget that I said it has been years since I've had sushi?"

"Why so long?" I inquired.

She gave a sad smile. "I guess I just haven't had a reason. I'm sure you noticed I don't leave town often. I prefer the calm and quiet."

"Could have fooled me. You've been so comfortable, I feel like you do this every weekend."

"Well, dear, I haven't always been this way."

I wasn't sure how far to pry, but, now that I had Mary talking, I wanted more. "So, what changed?"

She stayed silent for a moment as she stared into the distance, traveling miles away from our table with just one look. I waited patiently for her to find her way back. "People change. I learned how fleeting life could be, and I decided to abandon everything. I put all of my money into the antique shop and made it a home for myself."

Even though the answer was a bit abstract, I nodded in acceptance.

"You see my dear, life isn't about fulfilling yourself with materials and people that are fleeting and meaningless. Life is about finding your place in the world. It's about learning what makes you truly happy and pursuing it. It's about setting goals and meeting them." Her eyes shone with unshed tears. "If you take anything from our time together, please take that. You and only you are responsible for your own happiness."

I hated being reminded I was supposed to be moving on soon. I had been avoiding emails all day because I didn't want to see the notice of the bank deposit. I secretly prayed it would never show up. It made me feel like a crazy person. Of course I needed to move on. I was not a small town girl. I loved everything about the city, and I was eventually going to have to go back and find my own way. I needed to move to a large city where no one had ever heard the last name Burelli. Where I could use my money wisely, maybe purchase a home and get a part-time job. *I wonder if Callum would like living in the city.*

By the time I lugged my bags up the stairs to the apartment, I was ready to collapse, but as the door was open, the smell of fresh herbs and garlic permeated the air. Right away, I knew what Callum was making for dinner. Since my diet had flown out the window, I had been craving pizza. He had teased me about using my last wish to fulfill it, but I always rolled my eyes and ignored him. Seeing him in the kitchen rolling out dough and smelling the fresh sauce on the stove, I was more than happy with his choice. He winked at me, and the familiar butterflies rushed my tummy. I had somehow managed to keep thoughts of him at bay through the course of the day, but now my excitement reached new heights. He had made big promises about our evening, and I had been sure to behave so I could get what I deserved. Bar the cuss word that morning, I had been a freakin angel.

"How was your day?" Callum asked as he approached, floating over to us.

"It was great. This lady has been fooling us. She belongs in a city."

Mary walked by, shaking her head. "Belonged, dear. Those days are in the past. I much prefer my quiet, simple life."

Callum nodded. "I've been in a city. I have to agree

with Mary. The quality of life available here feels much better."

Not what I wanted to hear. "What? How do you figure? Its super inconvenient! You have to travel to the city to get anything you want. There's nowhere good to eat and zero nightlife. Where is the quality?" I tried to keep my temper in check, but it was difficult. I belonged in the city, but life without Callum wasn't an option. I took my bags to my room and flung them onto my dresser. Throwing myself onto the bed, I wrapped my pillow securely around my face and screamed. *Why does everything have to be so complicated? Why can't I have a normal life?* I hadn't spoken to my father in weeks, I was living hundreds of miles away from the place I had always called home, my mother had been alive and well yet I had spent my whole life thinking otherwise, and, on top of everything else I was madly in love with a freaking genie and there was no promise it could go anywhere. I flopped onto my back and gasped in surprise. Callum was in my room.

"What the f…"

"Don't." He cut me off before the word flew.

"You scared the crap out of me!"

"I apologize. I just came to check on you. You left rather quickly."

"I'm fine," I sighed.

"You can't lie to me, little sprite. I can hear you, remember?"

"Ugh, seriously! Get out of my head!"

Callum chuckled. "It's not my choice. You invite me when you think of me."

"I know, I know." As amazing as I thought it would be to have a partner who could read my mind, I was wrong. Some of my thoughts did not need to be overheard, especially by him.

"Where you a good girl today?" That simple question knocked all of the frustration clear out of my system and made my pussy spasm in excitement. "I love it when you blush like that," he continued to tease. "There is some time before dinner to paint your bottom with that same beautiful blush if you were naughty today."

I shook my head. A naughty girl spanking was not what I wanted. Not at all. "I was good. I swear."

His mouth quirked in a half smile. "I hoped you would say that. Come here." He pointed at the floor directly in front of him.

Scrambling off the bed, I found my place. I stood staring at his abs with my hands behind my back, but I couldn't keep still. I shook with anticipation. He put a finger under my chin and brought my lips to his. "Good girl." We settled into a sensual kiss, our lips brushing against one another's. Wrapping my arms up around his neck, I pulled him closer. This was what I needed. Getting lost in his kiss was the cure for my anxiety.

The timer on the oven beeped, and I stomped my feet in frustration. "How is it done already?" I whined. Thankfully, he snapped his fingers and pulled me back in. *Okay, so maybe having a magical boyfriend who can read my mind is a good thing.*

Chapter Nine

"That was the best pizza I've ever had. Oh my God, I am so full." I groaned in satisfaction as I leaned back in my seat. I felt as though I had gained ten pounds in one day. Each meal had been better than the last, and I had stuffed myself. "I can't remember the last time I ate like this."

"It's good for you. You could use a little meat on your bones." Callum pinched my thigh under the table, making me squeak.

"You two behave. I'm going down to Able's for poker night," Mary announced. My stomach flipped. I had never been in the apartment alone with Callum. He made it feel like we were alone, but I would be able to fully relax with Mary gone.

Rounding the table, Mary kissed me on the head. "Happy Birthday, dear. I had a wonderful day with you. Thank you." She laid her plate next to the sink and slipped her shoes on. "I won't be back for hours. Bye" Her parting words made Callum and I laugh out loud at her forwardness.

"I think it's safe to say she's not worried."

"She shouldn't be. She may be my mother, but I am an adult, and she doesn't get to boss me. It's not her job," I argued.

Callum sat back and crossed his arms over his chest. "Not her job, huh? Then whose job is it?"

My face heated. "I believe that's your department, Sir."

A feral growl rumbled through him, and the purple of his eyes began to sparkle. "Come here."

Each time he gave a command, my pussy flooded my panties with arousal. He didn't have to ask. With a snap of his fingers, he could do anything he pleased to my body, but sometimes I had to make the decision to obey or not. It empowered me and made me crave the moments when I was able to submit to him.

The table between us disappeared, and I stood up in front of him. Taking my hands, he penetrated me with a look so deep I couldn't move. "I believe, I made you a promise, did I not?"

Why did that sound so dangerous? This man had done things to me I had never allowed anyone to do. He had touched me in ways that would have literally gotten anyone else killed if my father found out, but, more than that, he made me ache for it. "Yes, Sir," I whispered.

"And what was that promise my little sprite?"

"That you were going to give me a birthday memory that would last the rest of my life."

"Indeed. I know you don't like to talk about it, but the truth is we aren't sure where either of us will be next year or in the years to follow."

"Please don't," I begged. "I can't think about that. Not tonight."

"I know it's hard for you, but it's important. I want you to let yourself go for me tonight. I want you to relax and allow me to take charge. I want you to feel the way I command your body here, here and here." He touched my forehead, chest, and unapologetically snaked his hand beneath my skirt, fluttering his fingers against the gusset of my soaked panties. The touch was so light it could have almost gone unnoticed, however, I was acutely aware of everything he did. “Do you trust me?”

“With everything I am, Sir.”

“Good girl. It’s time for your spanking.”

Tugging my arm slightly, he pulled me across his lap. Lap? I wrenched backward to see what was happening. Sure enough, the cloud at his waist was gone. In its place was all man. Hips to feet, he was all there. His chest was bare as always, but he wore light washed jeans. He couldn’t look any sexier. I looked up at his face, and he winked.

“I-is it all there?” I timidly gestured to where his cock should be.

He gave a sad smile and shook his head. “Some things even genies can’t do, but I will make sure you do not miss it. I promise.”

With a sigh, I lay over his knees. It was a wholly new feeling, and a good one. My side was pressed snugly against his muscled abs, and I could feel his warmth. One arm held me securely, and I heard the snap of his fingers just before my pants and panties disappeared. Crossing one ankle over the other, I squeezed as tight as I could. I was already dripping wet, but the intimacy of this position magnified it. Embarrassing to think I could be leaving a wet mark on his pants.

His hand settled on the back of my knee and dragged slowly up and around my bottom before descending down the other side. “What I wouldn’t give to be able to claim you as mine, sprite.”

“I’m already yours, Sir.”

“That you are, my girl, that you are.” The tickle of his fingers on my inner thigh coaxed my legs open, giving him full access to all of me, and he took it. With his hand pressed into the seam of my pussy, I moaned in delight. “You are so wet,” he murmured appreciatively. “Is this all for me?” I looked back in time to see him put his finger to his lips to taste my offering in one of the hottest moments I had ever experienced. My face burned with embarrassment as he opened his eyes and regarded me for a moment. "You are so sweet, my little sprite. I can't wait to have you pinned on your back as I take my fill."

Words escaped me, and I felt the need to look away. As soon as I did, the first smack fell on my vulnerable bottom before he rubbed the sting away. Moaning, I pressed my bottom into his hand, silently begging for more. He did not disappoint, repeating the pattern over and over. Spank, caress, spank, caress, back and forth, up and down. The pressure in my core built when the caresses changed to him exploring my sex with his fingers. I whimpered in need as I pressed against him, trying to get more.

"Not yet, naughty girl." His fingers disappeared and the spanking continued. I was on fire, inside and out, my bottom burning from crest to sit spots. Again, his fingers renewed their exploration, this time dragging the moisture toward my most secret area. Ass play had always been off limits, but body sang for him. He massaged my ring, bringing more and more moisture to my bottom hole. Without warning, he pressed his finger to the entrance. Instinctively, I tensed and tried to get away. Clicking his tongue, he laid some intense smacks to the backs of my thighs, making me cry out.

"You don't get to close yourself off to me. All that you are, is mine and mine alone."

Whimpering, I forced myself to relax. The pressure built until the tip of his finger glided into my ass. Neither of us moved. It was a show of pure dominance. He would give, and I would take, and there was nothing I could do about it.

My body fell limp over his lap before he removed his probing finger, leaving me equally relieved and frustrated.

Wanting to feel him inside me, I would take it any way I could get it at this point. Reading my mind, he inserted two fingers inside my pussy, making me gasp and release a long, low moan of pleasure.

"Music to my ears, my sweet. I look forward to making you scream, but you are not allowed to come yet. Mind your manners."

His edict confused me. "What? I can't come? But…"

The arm that had held me still disappeared, and his hand fell hard upon my scorched bottom. He spanked over and over while simultaneously pumping his fingers in and out of my channel. "Your only response is, 'Yes, Sir.' And if you come before I allow it, you will be a very sorry girl." His threat made me shiver, but his fingers never stopped. I had no idea how to hold back, but I had a sneaking suspicion disobeying would not be the best course of action.

His fingers slipped from my core and headed straight for my clit. If he put a modicum of pressure on my little bundle of nerves, I was going to lose control. Thankfully, he only swirled around it making it harden more. My body screamed in need. I could feel the orgasm building. When he decided to allow it, I was going to explode.

"I think you are ready, how about you?" He knew exactly how primed my body was. My pussy contracted around his fingers.

"Yes, I am so ready."

"Hmm, maybe you need to wait a little longer."

"What? No! Why?" I panicked. "I need it. Please, let me come."

His silence drove me mad as he made teasing figure eights around my core and clit. All of the wiggling and movement did nothing to get him to put out the fire he had so expertly stoked.

Growling in frustration, I held back all of the nasty

things I wanted to call him, my brain in a sexual haze. But cursing at him would not help my cause. "Oh my God, Callum. Please!"

His touches stopped altogether. His hand appeared in front of my face, and he snapped his fingers. All of a sudden, I lay on my back in my bed, no not my bed, the bed from my dreams. But this wasn't a dream, was it? I couldn't recall falling asleep. Attempting to sit up, I was halted by the tether attached to my wrists. I gave a cursory pull, but it proved fruitless. The same with my ankles. I was tied spread-eagle to the bedposts, stark naked. Never having been stripped in front of him, I flushed in embarrassment. I had never been self-conscious about my body, either, but this position was less than flattering, the room was bathed in light, and I didn't even know where Callum was.

Moisture pricked my eyes as I scanned the room for him, afraid. Appearing next to me he caught a tear just as it escaped. "Why are you crying?"

I shook my head not wanting to admit to my fear.

"Don't lie to me." His voice darkened, the warning clear.

"I didn't know where you went." I gave him a half-truth, hoping it would assuage him.

"I was here the whole time. I would never bind you and leave. Do you trust me?"

"Yes." My entire body shook. I couldn't identify if it was fear or anticipation of what was to come, but my discomfort was obviously clear to Callum.

"Tell me what's going on in that beautiful head of yours."

Biting my lip I held on as long as I could, but he was relentless. His stubbornness could outlast mine a thousand times over. "I... when I didn't see you, I got scared."

"Of what, my sweet?"

"Being alone." The last piece of the truth tumbled out of me.

Gently, he pressed his hand to the side of my face, and I nuzzled in, accepting the comfort. "I will stay with you for as long as I am permitted, little sprite." Leaning in, he took my mouth. The physical connection calmed my anxiety. He roamed my body with his hands, brushing against the stiff peaks of my breasts. It took no time at all for the pressure in my sex to build again. "Please, let me come."

"You know I love to hear you beg, but you have been missing a key component."

I wracked my mind, trying to figure out what the heck he talked about. I replayed the last twenty minutes in my head as he teased my body. His hands zeroed in on my nipples ,and he pinched. I hissed at the sharp pain traveling through my body, but then I realized what had been missing. "Sir! Sir! Pretty please let me come, Sir."

His proud smile gave me hope, and he floated to the end of the bed. Hovering over me, he took in my naked form, making me want to hide.

"Good girl," he praised before lowering his mouth onto my sex. With one swipe of his tongue, my toes curled and my entire body tensed as I screamed out the most intense orgasm I had ever experienced. He hummed in approval, and the vibrations rocked my body with aftershocks of pleasure.

Just as quickly as they had appeared, my tethers were gone, and I cuddled into his arms. Sex satiated, sore, and as content as could be.

"Not bad for round one," he announced.

"Round one? There's more?" The way I felt, I couldn't imagine being able to do that again, but I was not averse to letting him try.

"Oh, baby. I have barely begun. When I am finished with you, you won't be able to form a coherent thought. You will be lucky if you are able to walk tomorrow."

Whimpering in anticipation, I closed my eyes and lay against his chest. "I'm looking forward to it, Sir."

"Me too, little sprite. You are one delectable woman, my delectable woman."

"You are mine just as much as I am yours, Sir."

"I suppose you're right in that regard," he sighed.

Without thinking, I smacked his chest. "You suppose?"

Grabbing my wrist, he pinned my arm above my head. "You are a very naughty little girl."

Opening my eyes, I took in the scene. We were back in my room and even in the small bed., Callum had managed to sleep behind me. Pressing myself backward, I pulled his arm tightly against my naked breasts. His skin brushed my oversensitive nipples, making me shiver.

"What's wrong, little sprite? Didn't you get enough?" Callum's voice was husky with sleep.

Pressing my legs together I winced. A pinch to my backside guaranteed I needed to keep my sass to myself. "Ow! I had plenty, thank you very much."

"Good." He nuzzled my neck, making me giggle.

I rolled over in his arms to face him. "How did you know about the room?"

"What room?"

"The room in my dreams."

"I'm not following, sweetheart."

"The room we, um, played in last night. It wasn't my room, but I have seen it before, in my dreams."

Callum's face turned pensive. "It's my chamber. You dreamt about my room?"

"I guess. I have dreams about you almost every night, and every single one has happened there."

He shook his head slowly, a look of awe clouding his features. "Many things between the two of us have made me believe we have a unique connection, but that's the most telling by a long shot."

Hope swelled in my heart. As much as I didn't want to set myself up for heartbreak, every time he made comments like that I felt like we stepped one step closer to a future together.

Callum snapped his fingers, and we were in his room, once more. "Why didn't we just stay here last night?"

"I moved us, once you fell asleep. Having women in our chambers is not against code, but it is frowned upon. I have never brought anyone else here."

I crossed my arms and pursed my lips. "Did you have nights like that with anyone else?" I hoped he wouldn't answer. I didn't want to know.

Mimicking my stance, he stared me down. "You know the answer to that."

I bit my lip and blinked slowly. "No, I don't"

He didn't answer with words, he answered by snapping his fingers and sending me facedown over the side of the bed.

"No! No, no, no! I don't want a spanking, Sir, please!" My pants and panties slowly slid off my waist and skimmed over my bottom. "Please!"

"Do you trust me?"

"Yes! I swear I do." I panicked, my bottom so sore from the repeated spankings I had gotten the night before I felt it every time I moved. I did not want another one.

"Are you lying to me?"

"No! God, no! I would never. Please, Sir. Please don't spank me." Tears pricked the backs of my eyes.

"Stop. Take a breath and relax. I want you to think really hard about the question you asked me. Think hard about that trust. Do you think I could honestly share what we did last night with anyone else?"

I laid my head down on the bed and lost all composure. Sobs wracked my body as I realized the implication of my question. My jealousy had come to a head, and I might as well have slapped him in the face. The hold loosened, and I crawled onto the bed, wrapping myself in the fetal position. Callum's warm body engulfed me from behind. "Shh, my girl. You will be okay. I simply needed to make a point. You understand now, don't you? You are the only one for me, Fiona. It was written long ago that you and I would be soul mates. I knew it from the first time I laid eyes on you. I tried to ignore it, to suppress the feeling for fear I was wrong. But everything has happened so fast, and I cannot deny it any longer. Fiona, I need you to make your third wish."

I threw myself off the bed, backing away from him quickly as if he were a snake about to strike. Words escaped me, but I shook my head vigorously.

"Listen to me. I am not wrong about this. You are my one. You are her, and we are wasting time."

"You don't know that. You can't. What happens if I'm not? I can't go on without you. I won't."

"That's another reason we can wait no longer. You depend on me, and if I am wrong, which I am not, the longer I remain with you the more difficult it would be for us to say good-bye."

"No! Do you hear me? I'm not ready. I will never be ready! I need you. I have never needed anyone else, ever. I rely on myself because other people let me down, but not you. You're different, and I know you will never let me down. Please Callum, I… I love you." My knees shook as the terrifying phrase flew from my lips. The harsh reality I had not said that to anyone else in my life slapped me across the face.

He scooped me into his arms and held me close. "Okay, okay. Calm down please, sprite. Breathe with me." He modeled what he wanted me to do with slow, steady breaths, and I followed his lead. "Good girl, in and out. No more talk about wishes for today."

I sniffled. "Thank you. I'm sorry."

"There is nothing to apologize for. You deserve my apology, though. It's not right for me to ask you to use a wish. My mission is to serve you and keep you safe. The wishes are yours and yours alone."

"What if I wish for your freedom? Can I do that? In all of the stories you can!"

He shook his head slowly. "I'm sorry, little sprite. That is one of the myths that goes with the lamp. I am not permitted to free myself. Only my true love has that power. You hold that power, only not in the way you would like."

"This sucks, you know that?" I pouted. It all seemed so unfair, and I silently cursed all the damn writers who misled the whole world!

"I would have to agree with you."

"We should probably go back, my m... Mary might get worried."

"She won't even know we are gone. It hasn't been long enough. What's your aversion to calling her your mother? Don't you think you've punished her enough?"

"I'm not ready for that, either," I muttered not wanting to have this conversation.

"Okay, little sprite. Let's get breakfast, shall we?"

Food sounds safe. "Food sounds good." I nodded, and

,with a snap of his fingers, he moved us back into my little bedroom.

Setting me down, he allowed me a few steps before stopping me. “Little sprite, I need you to know something.”

I turned around to give him my full attention.

“I love you, too.”

Chapter Ten

Mary sat at the table with a cup of coffee, making me giggle. "What happened to caffeine is addicting and bad for your body and all that?" I sassed.

Callum came up behind me and smacked my butt, hard.

"Ow! What was that for?"

"Behave yourself."

"I...I didn't do anything!" I argued as I made my way to the coffeemaker, rubbing my tender bottom.

Shaking his head, he took his seat next to Mary.

"Good morning, you two. Did you have an enjoyable evening?"

"Mmmmm," I moaned.

Mary stared at me. A blush crept up my face as I realized what she probably thought. "I moaned about the coffee, not the evening," I mumbled.

Callum erupted in laughter.

"Really, Mr. Prim and Proper?" I fell into the seat next to him and cringed in pain. My bottom ached inside and out.

"Sore, little sprite? Maybe you want to remember that before throwing out more sass. We can go back to my chambers in the blink of an eye."

Mary shook her head. "That's enough, you two."

I sighed in relief. *Mom to the rescue.*

"You're right. It was out of line to speak to your

daughter like that in your presence. Please forgive me," Callum apologized.

Mary reached for his hand and gave it a squeeze. "I need to talk to you two."

Callum turned his hand over, engulfing Mary's, and I watched my mother fight back tears. Right away, I remembered Mary's emotional demeanor the day before. I had chalked it up to spending the first birthday ever with her daughter, but that didn't appear to be the case.

"What's wrong?" I pulled my feet up to rest on the seat of my chair, hugging my knees to my chest, trembling with fear and anxiety. Callum dragged my chair closer and rested his hand on my knee. The simple act gave me something to focus on, and the quivering stopped altogether.

"I went to the doctor last week." She paused, searching for words. "There's really no easy way to say this. I don't want to put this on you, but I have no choice. My cancer is back."

My heart dropped. "Cancer? Back? What are you talking about?"

Mary stared at the table as she spoke. "After you were born, I was diagnosed with ovarian cancer. They removed my uterus and, after a round of chemotherapy, they told me I was in remission. It came back a couple of years ago. This time, they found it in my breasts. I did four rounds of chemotherapy and radiation. I thought about taking my own life during that time more than anyone should ever have to. I begged God to let me die. The only thing keeping me going was wanting to get the store ready to sell so you wouldn't have to deal with any of my mess after I died. The last thing I wanted was for you to find out about me and my death and then have to worry about my debts and assets in the same breath. I wanted you to know how much I loved you and nothing more. After the fourth round, all of the scans came back clear. Last week, I wasn't so lucky. The cancer is in my brain. The prognosis is bleak, and I simply refuse to live out the rest of my days pumping poison into my body. I want to enjoy the time I have left."

Tears streamed down my face as she continued. I wanted to scream and cry. This could not be real. I had just met my mother and was getting to know her. Now, after living my entire life thinking my mother was dead, I was actually going to have to deal with that death? No, this couldn't be real. Hysterics consumed me, and I lost all "composure. "What do you mean? You aren't going to fight? You have to fight!" I slammed my palms on the table.

Mary shook her head, "I can't, baby. I can't do that again. Please, don't ask me to go through that again."

"Callum do something!" I glared at him expectantly, but when his own tears fell, I knew his answer. It was against the rules. I couldn't take it and collapsed on the spot. Mary and Callum were at my sides in a moment, sandwiching me in their loving embrace. I turned into the arms of my mother and wept. "Please, don't leave me again," I begged, knowing full well I was being unfair. Mary hadn't asked for any of this. No one would.

"I'm so sorry, dear. So very, very sorry. I was selfish to ask you to stay. I should have anticipated this and made you go home to your father. You could have lived your life never having known I was your mother. It would have saved you so much pain."

"No, please don't say that. Please. I have learned so much here with you and Callum. I've learned how great life can be when you get out of your comfort zone. I've learned how real people live. I've learned what love and family feel like. I learned how to love. I love you, Mom. I'm so thankful for everything, and I am going to stay by your side through the whole thing. If there's something we can do we, will fight. You won't have to be alone ever again. I promise."

Mary squeezed my hand tight as she shook with sobs. The entire time, Callum stayed silent. His touch and presence gave me the strength to finally say everything I needed to say. "I don't want to lose you again," I choked out.

There, in the middle of the threadbare carpet of a tiny one bedroom apartment, I realized how little everything in my life meant. The only things that mattered were the irreplaceable people, unconditional love, feelings of belonging and acceptance, and a sense of purpose. My life finally had purpose. I worked hard every day. I had even begun to enjoy it. The pride filling me when I accomplished a task inspired me to move to the next. Seeing the tattered shop almost fully restored gave me the nudge I needed to get my sore body moving each morning. The quality time spent with my mom and Callum made each tedious minute worth it. Now, in one morning, all of those feelings had been shattered. My mother was dying and no one could stop it. The shop would be sold, Callum would eventually have to move on, and I would be alone. Again. I cried until I had no tears left. Never had a situation felt so hopeless.

I woke to the gentle touch of a finger to my cheek. Opening my sore, dry eyes, I saw my mother. Face puffy, eyes red rimmed, she had never looked weaker. Mary had been a driving force for the past few weeks, and now I could see only the sickness.

"Please, don't look at me like that, dear," Mary begged. "Don't make me sorry I shared this with you. I wanted to be fair. I wanted to make sure you were prepared for what was to come. You need to make plans for your future. We need to tie up all of the loose ends so you can be free to live your life the way you deserve to live it."

I listened carefully, soaking in the sound of her voice and the faint floral smell unique to her. I wanted these memories of my mother. If I only had a short time left with her, then I needed to make the most of the time I was given. I nodded in acceptance. "Okay, Mom."

Mary's breath hitched, and she covered her mouth. "Thank you," she whispered as she fought the emotions warring on her tired face. I sat up and wrapped my arms around her .

"We are going to make the best of the time we have. Let's do everything you want to do. I have the money! We can travel! See the world. There is no limit." Excitement filled me. I could use my money I to make my mother's last days the best of her life, and I wasn't going to waste any time.

Mary pulled back and braced her hands on either side of my face. "We don't need money to enjoy our time. I am just so thrilled you are here with me. You and Callum are a blessing."

"But we can go anywhere, do anything. There has to be something on your bucket list."

Mary smiled, "Well come to think of it…"

I looked out the door of the plane, trying not to freak out. I was attached to a strange man and about to jump to my death because of all the things she could have chosen, my mother decided she wanted to experience skydiving. I was deathly afraid of heights, but the devil himself couldn't keep me from jumping out of that plane.

"On my count, we will fall out of the plane together. Ready?" the man yelled near my ear, barely audible over the loud whir of the plane engine. The voice in my head screamed at me to stay in the plane where I belonged.

Mary, on the other hand, was ready. Every time I glanced in her direction she would grin and give two thumbs up. I should have listened to Callum…

"No! Absolutely not! Neither one of you is jumping out of an airplane while I am around."

"We already have confirmed reservations. It's all paid for, and my mother is dead set on going."

"I said no. End of discussion. It is my mission to serve you and keep you safe. Allowing you to jump from a plane is the opposite of that. No."

I rolled my eyes at his stubborn protectiveness. Even though I had not liked the idea myself, hearing him protest so vehemently made me more determined to do it. Callum closed the distance between us and fisted the hair at the back of my neck. "I forbid you to jump out of an airplane, do you understand me?" He didn't give me the chance to respond before he claimed my mouth in a bruising kiss. His hold on my hair sent pinpricks of pain through my body, instantly turning me on. Rising on tiptoe, I wrapped my arms around his neck and returned his passion as best as I could. The whole time I kissed him, I knew. I was going to jump out of a plane and then he was going to spank my butt.

"One! Two! Go!" the instructor yelled before he nudged me forward and I plunged toward the ground at top speed. The air moved so quickly around me my scream caught in my throat. All I could do was pray the parachute would open and this nightmare would be over.

~

"Oh my God! Why did I wait all these years to do that?" Mary bounced in excitement. She had been reciting the same phrase over and over again since we had landed on the ground. As soon as I was unhooked from the instructor, I lay on the ground and wept. It had been an exhilarating adventure, but I was thankful to have made it alive. I would never do that again.

"You are in so much trouble, young lady." Callum's voice echoed in my head. He knew where we were. He knew I had disobeyed. My butt was toast.

"Thank you so much, Fi! I am so glad you talked me into doing that. I would have never gone through with it otherwise."

"You're welcome, Mom."

"What's wrong, dear? You have been so quiet. Is everything alright?"

"Yeah, it's fine. I'm fine."

"Fiona, I know you better than that already. You can't lie to me."

I kept my eyes trained on the road as I drove.

"Is everything okay with you and Callum?" She spoke slowly, as if afraid to ask the question.

I bit my lip. "Yeah, well, kinda. I don't know. We are probably fine."

"He didn't want us to do this today, did he?"

Glancing at my mother out of the corner of my eye, I shook my head. "No. Not at all and… I'm just not sure what I'll be facing when we get home."

Mary sighed and rested backward in her seat. "Did he ever tell you about the time I was arrested for skinny dipping in a public pool?"

Hearing stories about the dumb things my mother had done made me feel less like a failure and more… normal. "Nope. I haven't heard that one."

"Oh, he was so mad at me. A friend and I had been drinking, and it was hotter than hell outside. It was the middle of the night, and there was no one around, so we snuck into the pool. We weren't there for even ten minutes before the police showed up. He spanked me good for that stunt. He could care less about anything except that I had put myself in danger. It's his 'mission to serve and protect.'" Mary made finger quotes in the air and lowered her voice in a poor impression of Callum's.

I burst out in laughter. "He has said that to me a few times."

"Oh dear, he said it to me every day. I was so reckless. It's hard to believe I survived young adulthood and, yet, now a sickness is going to cause my death. It's hard to wrap my mind around."

I reached across the center console and squeezed her hand. "It sucks, I agree, but can we please not go there? Not today"

Nodding, Mary relaxed again.

"Wh-what did he do to you?" My curiosity got the best of me.

"It was the worst spanking he ever gave me." Her words did not match the wistful look in her eyes.

"Mom, did you ever… I don't know how to ask this. Did you ever like it when he spanked you?"

"Heavens no! It hurt terribly, and I hated disappointing him. Callum was like the daddy I never had."

I blushed, "Oh, okay."

"Listen, sweetheart, you and Callum have something special. I see it. He is head over heels in love with you."

"That doesn't mean anything if the universe doesn't agree."

Mary looked at me, confused.

"You know, the whole third wish thing? If he and I are

destined to be together then, after my last wish, he will be free, but, if not, he will disappear from their lives."

"I have no idea what you are talking about, dear."

Stopping at a red light, I turned to face her. "He never told you about all that?"

"No, he didn't tell me much about himself, really. He focused on me and trying to help me get better, but no one could get through to me at that age. I was dumb and so selfish."

The light turned green, and I had to continue driving. It gave me a moment to think through what I had learned. Why would Callum be so different with me than he had been with my mother?

"Did you know he has served our family for six generations?"

"No."

"Isn't that weird? Why would he tell me, but not you?"

"You are the one, and he knows it." Mary's entire demeanor brightened.

"He's said that, and I want to believe it so bad, but I'm scared. What if he is wrong? What if I make my last wish and he disappears? I can't deal with losing you and him both. I won't survive it."

"You need to trust him. He is a wise man, and he will never lead you to believe something untrue. He would rather die than hurt you."

She was right, but the risk was too great. I wasn't ready. Not yet. Not ever, if I had any say in the matter. As we pulled up to the shop, trepidation filled my stomach. I could see Callum watching through the window. His purple eyes glowed. I would pay dearly for my choice.

A lump formed in my throat as we got out of the car and went inside. Hands on his hips, he stood silently glaring at us.

"She did it for me, Callum. Go easy on her, will you?" Mary made her request as direct as possible, while keeping an air of respect.

"Mary, would you excuse us, please?" He snapped his fingers, transferring him and me directly to his chambers.

"Callum, I—"

"You directly disobeyed me."

"But—"

"You put yourself in danger."

"I'm fine! They are professionals."

"Did I or did I not forbid you to jump from a plane?"

"You did, but—"

"There is no but."

"I had to support my mother. Don't you understand that?"

"You could have supported her any other way! You did not need to jump out of an airplane!" he voice roared.

I had never seen him so upset before and, frankly, I was scared. Backing away a few steps, I gave myself a little bit of space to breathe.

"Don't look at me like that. I am not going to harm you. I would never even discipline you while in this state of mind." He sighed.

I trusted him. He had never hurt me before except to mete out well-deserved discipline, but he remained intimidating as hell.

"I brought us here because I needed to see where your head was at. You are not even slightly remorseful for your defiance. Does what I say mean nothing?"

"What? How can you even stand there and ask me that. You know how much I love you." I was so stunned he would even think to ask something like that, my anger bubbled just below the surface.

"Your actions do not match your words. You do know what happens if something happens to you don't you?"

"Yes! But nothing happened. You are being ridiculous."

"I see." He stood silently for a moment. "I think you need to spend some time thinking about your actions. Whether you agree with my decision or not is irrelevant at this point. You chose to do what I told you not to do, and that is what I want you to focus on. You are grounded. You may not leave the shop for any reason without my explicit permission." He raised his hands and snapped his fingers again, not allowing me to argue. I found myself in my room conveniently facing a corner.

"Ugh!" I stomped my feet and screamed. "You are such an egotistical asshole! Really? You're just going to banish me to my room like a naughty five-year-old? Well, screw you then!" I kicked the wall a few times before falling into my bed and screaming into my pillow.

"Fi? Dear? Are you okay?" Mary walked into the room.

"He grounded me! Can you believe that? I am a grown ass woman! He has no right!"

Mary sat on the bed and placed a calming hand on my knee. "Take a breath. You're not going to like what I have to say, but he's right."

"What? How? How can you even think that?"

"Because he loves you, and he has your best interests in mind. It's not about the plane anymore. It's about you choosing to trust and obey him. It's about putting everyone else to the side and putting him first. Even yourself. He would do anything for you. Would you do the same?"

"Of course, I would!"

"Then, show him."

I covered my eyes with my arm and took a few breaths to calm my growing frustration. "How?"

"How do you think? What would make him the happiest?"

I did know the answer, but it was a hard pill to swallow. The first time he had forbidden me from doing something I had my mind stuck on doing, I had completely disregarded him and his feelings. He was so strong and so solid, it was sometimes difficult to think I could hurt him. "I guess I'm grounded," I whined.

Mary nodded and stood. "Good, there's work to be done, anyway. Change into some work clothes and meet me downstairs."

I chuckled at Mary's retreating back. A few days after my twenty-third birthday, millions of dollars sitting in my bank account, and I chose to stay in this tiny apartment, grounded for not being obedient to my genie boyfriend. *What a crazy thing life is.*

Chapter Eleven

My knees ached as I continued to sand the wooden floor beneath me. The machine we had rented did not reach into all the nooks and crannies of the store, so the only option was to do it by hand.

Mary came out from the back room, drying her hands. "I'm going to take a break and get dinner in the oven. Great work, dear. Almost done?"

I wiped the sweat from my brow. It was so god-forsakenly hot, but we made progress. "With this spot. Then I need to do behind the counter."

Nodding, Mary headed up to the apartment. "Remember your restriction," she teased in a singsong voice.

I rolled my eyes and went back to the job at hand. I had been pissed about his edict but came to terms with the fact he was making a point and I needed to prove my love and trust. "Actions speak louder than words," I chanted to myself.

"Indeed they do." His deep voice came from behind me.

Dropping my chin to my chest, I took a deep breath. If he was here, it meant he had calmed down, and I was going to have to face my comeuppance.

I sat back on my haunches and turned to face him. The smirk on his face lightened my mood immensely. His disappointment weighed heavy on me, and to see him smile offered relief.

"I hear you have thought about what I said, then?"

"Yes, Sir." I got to my feet and adopted the most contrite pose I could. "I am so sorry for my behavior. I'm sorry for jeopardizing myself, which, in turn, put you in a crappy situation." I looked into his eyes, hoping he would recognize sincerity. "More importantly, I'm sorry for disrespecting your wishes and acting like it was no big deal."

Callum grasped the back of my neck and pulled me into a hug. "Thank you, little sprite," he spoke into the hair on the top of my head. His warm breath sent tingles down my spine.

A loud crash came from upstairs, startling us both. I instinctively turned to run in the direction of the sound, but Callum transferred us both and, instantly, I stood in front of one of my worst nightmares. Mary lay unmoving on the floor of the kitchen amidst some broken glass. Running to her side, I screamed at Callum to call 9-1-1.

"Mom! Mom!" I screamed as I nudged her prone body. The glass around her disappeared, and I scooted up to Mary's face. Placing my hand on her cheek, I shook gently. "Mom! Wake up. The ambulance is coming. Please wake up!" Tears streamed down my cheeks as I pleaded with my mother to open her eyes.

The paramedics showed up, and I backed against the wall to get out of their way. Callum had disappeared from sight, but I could feel his presence. I watched the medics work. They wrapped her neck in a brace and strapped her onto a backboard as they checked her vitals and spoke in terms I did not understand. My hand was engulfed by an invisible force I knew had to be Callum. I wished he could be with me physically, but being seen by others was frowned upon in his world.

"Ma'am, we are taking your mother to Riverside Medical. Do you have anyone you can call?"

I shook my head. "I'm all alone." Saying it aloud was almost too much and my hand was squeezed to the point of pain. *No not alone, Callum is here,* I reminded myself. "I need to stay with her," I pleaded with the paramedic.

He gave a slight nod and indicated for me to follow them.

They carried Mary down the stairs and placed her onto a waiting stretcher then rolled her out to the waiting ambulance. I climbed into the rig next to the driver, buckled in, and folded my hands in my lap. Bowing my head, I closed my eyes and, for the first time in my life, I prayed. "Please let her be okay. Please. I need more time. Just a little more time."

Everything happened so fast that I didn't have time to process on the way to the nearby hospital. It was small but seemed to be well staffed and everyone was helpful and encouraging. I was numb, unable to form thoughts or sentences or even hear some of the things said. All I could think about was my mom. She had to be okay. Unable to answer most of the questions thrown at me, I was shoved off to the side as an orderly moved my mother through a pair heavy double doors, leaving me alone in the hall.

"Ma'am. If you will come with me, we can get some paperwork done, and I can show you to the waiting room," a kind nurse spoke to me in a comforting tone.

"I-I need to know she's okay. I need someone to tell me she is okay," I whispered, not taking my eyes off the sterile white doors.

"As soon as the doctors know anything, you will be informed. You are her daughter, correct?"

I nodded.

"Please come with me. The faster we get through the paperwork, the better things will be."

It didn't make any sense. What was paperwork going to do to wake up my mother? I needed to be with her not filling out her name and birthdate on forms. Hell, I probably didn't even know the information.

"I can't help."

"Okay, honey, let me take you to the waiting area."

I didn't want to move. What if my mom needed me? What if she called for me and I wasn't there? Anxiety clogged my throat, making it almost impossible to breathe.

"Breathe, sprite." Callum's voice penetrated the deep fog.

I turned in a circle trying to find him, but it was only me and the nurse in the hall.

"Focus on my voice and breathe. Do as you are told and allow the doctors to do their job."

"Yes, Sir," I whispered.

"I'm sorry?" The nurse asked.

"Oh, sorry, nothing." I turned back and followed the nurse.

"Good girl. I'm here. Focus on my voice," Callum continued "Breathe in, out, in, out," he instructed. Feeling him near, I found my breath. Commotion went on all around me, but I didn't pay attention to anything but his voice and doing what he said. *Even breaths in and out. In and out.*

I slept curled in a chair next to Mary's bed. It felt like

hours before the doctor came out and updated me. From what they could gather, Mary had passed out and banged her head on the way down. When the oncologist scanned her, they learned her prognosis was worse than they had thought. The cancer had spread like wildfire, devouring her brain. The doctors called it a miracle my mother was even still alive.

They kept Mary heavily sedated, but, after hearing my sad story, the nurses allowed me to stay by her side. I wanted to scream and cry and throw things as I dealt with my uncontrollable emotions, but I could not risk being kicked out. Callum popped in and out, but it was difficult with people checking on my mother every fifteen minutes. Falling asleep from sheer exhaustion had been my only saving grace.

"Fi?" My mother's weak voice came from the bed.

Jumping up, I grabbed her hand and squeezed. "Mom, I'm here."

Mary's glassy eyes met mine, and I couldn't help but let the tears fall. "Where am I? What happened?"

"We are at Riverside Medical. You passed out in the kitchen and hit your head." I tried to keep my voice calm and level, but I was so scared.

"It's the end, isn't it?" Mary asked.

"Please don't ask me questions like that, Mom. I can't…"

"The doctors are not hopeful, Mar." Callum materialized on the other side of the bed.

I scowled at him. I wanted her to rest. Stress wasn't going to help.

Mary nodded in resignation. "I knew it was coming, I just hoped I had a little longer." she squeezed my hand. "Thank you, dear."

I was taken aback. "For what? I didn't do anything."

"You've accepted me. It's all I ever wanted." She smiled weakly, her eyes closing.

"I love you, Mom. Close your eyes and rest. I will be here when you wake up," I coaxed, running the back of my hand down my mother's pale face.

Mary nodded and dozed off.

"Why would you tell her that?" I growled at Callum.

"She has the right to know, little sprite. This is not a surprise to her. Something tells me she guessed how bad it was and downplayed it for your sake."

Ignoring his reasoning, I charged forward with my anger. "She didn't need to know right this minute. You could have waited."

"Sprite, listen to me. You are the one who is not ready to accept it. I understand. Saying good-bye to my mother and father was one of the most difficult things I have ever had to do. For a long time, I held onto hope I would cross their paths again, but that hope was dashed when I learned of their deaths. They lived, long happy lives, my 'brothers and sister gave them many grandkids and years of happiness, and I missed all of it. I understand what you are feeling, and I am sorry, but we all have to accept what fate has in store for us. We cannot control it."

I dialed in closely to what he said. He didn't talk a lot about his family, and now I knew why. It still hurt him to be away from them. Rounding the bed, I scooted as close as I could to him, forcing him to put his arm around me. I rested my head on his chest and looked into his glowing eyes. "Thank you for sharing that with me. I know it was hard."

"I want to share everything with you, little sprite."

I sighed and took my mother's hand. "I just need a little more time…" That statement held so much weight. I needed time with my mother, and I needed time to decide what to do about my third wish. At the moment, all I could focus on was my mother's cold fingers laced in my hand and my man's warm bare chest pressed to my back. All of us attempting to transfer love and strength to one another.

"Do you need anything else?" I asked before leaving Mary's room.

"I'm fine, dear. You're smothering me!" Her chuckle was weak, but her spirits had stayed high. After two weeks in the hospital, she was just glad to be in her own room. Before they'd allowed her to go home, I had gotten a hospital bed and set up hospice care. She was visited often by a nurse, but I made it my job to keep her comfortable.

"I just want to make sure you're okay. Sheesh," I tossed out before heading out to the kitchen where Callum waited. He opened his arms, inviting me into my favorite place. Accepting his support, I collapsed in his strong embrace. "I'm tired."

"I know you are, little sprite. Why don't you take a nap?"

"I can't! What if she needs me?"

"The nurse won't be back for hours, but I will stay and make sure she is well taken care of."

"I can't. What if…"

" Listen to me. little girl. You are running yourself ragged, and you need to rest. I understand you want to care for your mother, and I understand your fears, but you cannot take proper care of her without allowing me to take proper care of you."

A tiny whine emerged from my lips, but he was right

"I will take you to my chamber where you will lie down and get some much-needed rest. You can sleep for hours and barely miss any time here. I promise to retrieve you should anything change with your mother."

"But..." I protested halfheartedly.

"The only butt you need to be concerned about is your own, and if you would like to take a nap with a stinging red bottom, I can make that happen."

Burying my face in his chest, I attempted to hide my blush, but Callum knew what words like that did to me. Even though I was beyond exhausted, his dominance still flipped my switch.

"I don't want a nap, but I will take you up on the other part," I boldly requested. I had never asked him for a spanking, but I needed one. It had been a long time since the two of us had any time alone together. He had tried to pull me away, but, even knowing the time separation between the two realms, it scared me to leave my mother. Mary was her same feisty self, but her health had declined quickly, and she wasn't even able to walk to the bathroom anymore. Her meds made her sleep a lot, and she had a hard time with most foods. Soon, her body would shut down completely and I wanted to be there in the last hours, the last minutes. Mary had spent so much time fighting for her life all alone. It made me sick to think I could have been here if my father hadn't been such a selfish prick.

Callum shook his head. "You are something else, you know that? Go nap." He lifted his hand and snapped me into his room. I stood pouting in the middle of the space.

"Fine, you big jerk!" I yelled, not caring if he could hear me or not. Flouncing over to the bed, I threw myself onto the soft pillows. They cradled my entire body, giving me the feeling of floating in the clouds. I closed my eyes and gave in to sleep.

"There's my good girl," Callum whispered in my ear.

Smiling, I nuzzled the pillow beneath my head. "I know you're awake, you little faker." He nipped my ear, and I giggled.

"Go 'way I'm sleepin'," I mumbled.

"Not anymore you're not. You're on my time, now. You know what that means?"

Flipping onto my back, I stretched out the last vestiges of sleep and nodded excitedly. "Yes, Sir." I knew exactly what it meant. Pleasure.

"I will give you control over one thing. You may orgasm whenever you are ready. You deserve it. My girl has worked way too hard lately. I'm so proud of you."

He snapped his fingers, and I was instantly naked and bound to the corners of his bed. My pussy gushed as I gave cursory tugs on the straps. Being bound for him was my second favorite position, my first being securely held over his knee.

A snap in the air broke the silence, right before the falls of my favorite flogger trailed up my body. The tickling sensation brought goose bumps to my skin, and my nipples puckered, reaching for the unique sting I knew would follow. Callum started slowly, raising and lowering the strands in a manner that made them thud against my skin.

An especially hard stroke landed on my thigh, taking me out of my mellow trance and making me squeak in surprise.

Callum's deep chuckle almost earned him a glare, but I was in no position to challenge him in any way. "You want more, sweet girl?"

"Oh yes, please, Sir. Lots more."

"Your wish is my command."

I sat up in a panic. Sweat covered me from head to toe, and my breathing was erratic. A panic attack. Looking around, I hoped to see I was still in Callum's room.

Hearing him say that phrase had frightened me into thinking I had accidentally spoken the forbidden words. Callum materialized beside me.

"What happened, little sprite? I could feel your angst."

I jumped into his arms, needing to feel he was really still there. "I had a nightmare. Well, it didn't start as one. It was a nice dream but then you said, 'Your wish is my command,' and it woke me up. I was scared I'd screwed up. I was scared you would be gone." I choked out the last words, and tears followed. I hadn't cried since the first day at the hospital, and I was so tired of being strong.

He held me in his arms, rocking back and forth. The motion and the steady beat of his heart had a calming affect unrivaled by anything or anyone. "I'm here, little sprite. It was only a dream. I'm not going anywhere. Even if you did make the third wish, I would still be here. You know what my wish is?" he asked. I did know, but I stayed silent. "I wish you would trust me."

"I do, Callum. I really do, but I'm scared."

"There is nothing to be afraid of. You are my future. We are going to spend the rest of our lives together. We will build a home and a family. I will make all of your dreams come true."

Sighing, I nodded. "Can we get through all of this with my mother, please?"

"The timing is up to you, little sprite. I can't force you to wish, it's…"

"Against code. I know I know. Everything helpful is against the damn code."

"Not everything," he smirked as he flipped me belly down in the air. "I find this very helpful." He pulled up my skirt and wedged my panties between my bottom cheeks.

"No no no!" I wiggled back and forth, but he had restricted my movement with his evil sorcery.

"Yes, yes, yes," he chanted back, punctuating his words with a smack of his hard palm. "Now, let's talk about how helpful this is. When is the last time you spouted a naughty word?"

"Ugh! Are you kidding right now?"

three more swats. Left, right, middle.

"Ow! Stop!"

Again. Left, right, middle.

"Okay, okay! It's been a long time!" I cringed, waiting for the next stinging blow.

"Oh, an answer, finally! Let's try another one. What naughty word did you say?"

"It slipped out," I whimpered.

He repeated the swats.

"Damn! Damn! I said damn."

"You did. Do I like that word?"

"No, Sir."

"Now you're getting it. Is that word befitting a lady?"

"No, Sir."

"What happens when my little sprite doesn't act like the well-behaved young lady I know she can be."

"I get punished, Sir."

"Yes, you do. So, here's what's going to happen. You are going to spell the word over and over again until I tell you to stop. Understand?"

I wasn't dumb. I knew this was going to be way more than a spelling quiz, but there wasn't much I could do, besides obey. "Yes, Sir."

"Good girl. Start whenever you're ready."

As soon as the first letter was out of my mouth, the spanking began in full force. If I stopped spelling, the spanks fell to the tenderest part of my upper thighs. After spelling the word over and over again, I swore to myself it would never happen again. I had no way to keep track of how many swats or how many times I spelled the wicked word, but by the end the letters forced out through choked sobs.

"Do you think this will help you remember what words should not be allowed to pass your beautiful lips?" His hand made gentle circles over my scorched flesh.

"Y-yes, S-sir." I hiccupped. "Will you h-hold me, p-please?" I felt rejected being suspended in the air as I was. My request was granted immediately and I was once again cuddled against Callum's chest. "I'm s-sorry. I was bad."

"You were not bad, little sprite. You said a naughty word, and you were punished. I would not have been so hard on you if I didn't think you needed it, but you did."

I couldn't argue his point. The pain had allowed me to release a lot of my stress. Now if only I could get him to… I jumped when he pinched the peak of my nipple through my shirt.

"Now, let's take care of you another way, shall we?"

Gently, he laid my back in the soft pillows and made the remainder of my clothing disappear. Biting my lip, I watched his body move into a horizontal position right above me.

"You relax like a good girl and let Daddy take away all of your stress."

Lowering his mouth to mine, he brushed my lips before shifting his mouth directly above my weeping sex. His fingers teased my nipples as his tongue did magical things to my pussy. It only took a minute before he brought me to the peak of pleasure. The real thing was always so much better than my dreams.

"We need to get you back to the apartment, sprite," Callum informed me before putting my clothing back in place.

I shook my head at him. "What about my panties?"

"I don't think you are permitted to wear those any longer. They get in my way."

"What?" I laughed. "You're a freakin genie. How does anything get in your way?"

He didn't answer.

With a wink and a snap, we were back in the kitchen of the apartment. My stomach grumbled, reminding me I had not eaten since breakfast. It was nearing dinner time so, after checking in on my mother, who slumbered peacefully, I busied myself making dinner for me and Callum.

Chapter Twelve

"Please, don't leave me, Mom. Please!" I begged the sleeping woman. Her health declined quickly. She could barely stay awake for more than a few minutes at a time and was on so many pain meds she no longer thought clearly. There were nurses on duty around the clock, but I had taken to sleeping on a small bed Callum conjured up. The tiny room didn't leave much space for me, but it was better than sleeping on the floor which is where Callum had found me a couple of nights ago. He got on my case about not asking for help, but asking him for anything was scary. I didn't want anything to be misconstrued as a wish.

"Fi, dear?" Mary turned her head in my direction.

"I'm here, Mom." I sniffled.

"Why are you crying?"

"I'm fine. Just tired. How are you feeling?"

"Oh, I'm peachy. If I could just keep my eyes open." She closed her eyes and sighed.

"What can I do, Mom? How can I make all of this worth it? What can I do for you?"

"You are doing everything, dear. I don't need more. I need to rest, but I can't do that until I see you are okay…" She fell asleep once again.

I folded my arms on the side of the bed, laid my head down, and sobbed. "I don't know what to do. I can't watch you like this anymore, but I don't know what to do to help you. How do I help you let go? How do I let you go?"

A warm presence pressed to my back, I could tell it was Callum from the way my body instantly reacted to his touch. With a nurse in the apartment twenty-four hours a day, he had to stay scarce, which of course made everything harder on me. He was my strength and my safe place. I needed him more now than I ever thought I would need another human being.

"I don't even know if she hears me. She can't stay awake long enough to talk about anything. I need her to tell me what she wants, what to do. I can't make these decisions on my own."

"You are not alone, little sprite. I'm right here, and you are strong enough to do anything you set your mind to."

Closing my eyes, I rested my head against his muscled torso. "If only I could see what you and my mom see in me."

"You will." Mary squeezed my hand slightly. "Listen to your man, dear. He's wise, and he loves you. My single wish is you find your place in the world and live life to the fullest. If only I could be around to see the amazing things the future holds for you. I know you will make me proud because you already have." Her breathing was labored and shallow. The creases in the corner of her eyes and mouth deepened, a sure sign the pain was bad.

"Do you want me to get the nurse, mom?" I jumped up, ready to act without listening, but something in Mary's eyes wouldn't let me go. "Mom?"

"I love you, sweetheart. I have loved and missed you your entire life. Please forgive me for letting him win." Her eyes clouded with tears.

"I forgave you a long time ago. I love you so much." I leaned over and kissed her forehead. Saying those words aloud brought more calmness to my heart than I had experienced since I learned about the diagnosis. I could see it had the same effect on Mary.

"Thank you, dear. You behave yourself. I'm going to go back to sleep."

Something inside told me this was my last opportunity to say what I needed to express to my dying mother. "Thank you, for everything." I laid my head gently on her chest and listened as her heart beat for the very last time.

"She's gone," the nurse announced gently.

I sniffled and nodded, but I did not move. The last few weeks had been so physically and emotionally draining I almost felt relieved. The pain lines in my mother's face softened and, if I didn't know any better, I would swear she was smiling.

"What am I gonna do with this place? It doesn't feel right to sell it. I worked so hard." I looked around the shop. The transformation was incredible, but it still was far from finished.

"So keep it." Callum shrugged. We hadn't really discussed any of the "after" stuff because I had not been able to mentally or emotionally handle anything regarding my mother's death, but it had been a couple of days since her death, and she had finally been laid to rest. I had come from the lawyer's office and spreading the ashes. My mother left everything to me, including over twenty-seven million dollars she had saved over the years. Hush money from my father. She had only used enough to get clean and buy the shop then opened an account and saved the rest for me. She lived this life so she could give me everything she had. Amazing how selfless she was. I respected her so much, but I also was upset she had not used the funds to take a little better care of herself. She did not have to break her neck getting the shop ready to sell or stress about it being foreclosed on. None of that mattered any more. She was gone and there was nothing anyone could do about the past.

"I can't keep it."

"Why not?"

"I don't know how to finish fixing it up. I don't know the first thing about running a business, and I belong in the city."

"The city isn't far and what do you need to know? It's all here." He swept his arms, indicating the boxes of clean merchandise ready to go up onto the shelves.

My mother hadn't known the first thing about running a business either, but she had loved every minute of working in her shop. She bought and sold things that caught her eye with no real rhyme or reason. She was not out to make millions, she just wanted to live her life.

I had millions. I didn't need the money from the shop to live, but I also had no real direction in which to go. I missed the city. The sights, the smells, the people, all so different than the country. But the country had grown on me significantly. The fresh air and the open spaces were so refreshing. I loved all of the plants and flowers, and life moved a lot slower. Meeting the owners of the other shops and getting to know them a bit had been an adventure in itself. Each of them had their own story and had welcomed me into the town like a long lost child, especially after finding out Mary was indeed my mother. Leaving was going to be difficult.

"I need to move on. I promised her I would find my place and be happy. I don't care if it takes the rest of my life to fulfill that promise, I'm determined to do it."

Callum wrapped his arm around my shoulders. "How

do you know this is not your place? Think about the last few weeks. Think about how much you have changed. Right here, in this shop, with me, this is where you belong, little sprite. This *is* your happy."

I was silent for a long moment. I had no argument. Once again, my man was right. "But what do I do about all of this? I can't finish this on my own."

"You do have a wish left, you know."

I closed my eyes and took some deep breaths to fend off the anxiety.

"You still don't trust me," Callum expressed with disappointment.

He couldn't be more wrong. I trusted him with every fiber of my being. Pulling out from under his arm, I turned to face him. "Genie, I'm ready for my last wish."

His pleased smile gave me the confidence I needed to follow through.

"I wish this store was fully restored to exactly what my mother dreamed it could be." Closing my eyes, I listened for the words that could potentially be the last thing he ever said to me. A soft kiss landed on my lips. I opened my eyes in time to watch him raise his hand into the air.

"Your wish is my command." With a snap, the room around me morphed. The shelves filled with merchandise, the racks rebuilt, and clothes hung up. The dark wood floors gleamed with polish and the glass of the display cases clear as crystal. It was as if the store had been picked out of a magazine, yet it all felt so warm and familiar. There was only one small problem, Callum was gone. I saw no trace of him anywhere.

Running up the newly finished stairs, I slammed open the door. The apartment had morphed also. Everything new and updated, exactly like the space I always imagined myself living in… but still no Callum.

"Callum! Callum Graham! Where are you? Please, don't do this! If you are playing some kind of sick joke, I swear to God I am going to kick your ass!" I stomped my feet in frustration. He couldn't be gone. He promised me, and I believed him. I trusted him like he wanted me to. So where the hell was he?

Heading downstairs, I went into the office. A new computer replaced the dinosaur that used to occupy the entire surface of the desk, but I noticed little else. I charged straight toward the secret door, on a mission. When I hit the wall, nothing happened. It didn't swing open as it had in the past, and I could not even see cracks or creases where the door had been. It was a solid wall.

"What the hell?" I screamed as I pounded on the wall. "Why won't you open? There's a whole room back here. I saw it!"

Leaving the office, I walked around back to where the room should be. In the wall was a large metal door. A safe of some sort, with a keypad for entry. "Great. How the hell am I supposed to know what the code is?"

Taking a wild stab in the dark, I punched in my birthdate. The red light turned green and a click came from the inside. Pulling the door open. I held my breath. The uncertainty of what could be in there scared me half to death, but I had to find Callum.

To my dismay, it was empty. "What do you need a huge safe for, if you have nothing to put in it?" I walked the perimeter, thoroughly confused. With the configuration of the store, this space must replace the old witch's room I had found Callum's bottle in. But why get rid of it? Why the safe? And where the hell was Callum?

Panic bubbled right below the surface. "This can't be happening. He has to be here somewhere. I need him. Callum!" I let out a strangled scream before collapsing into a heap on the floor. My worst nightmare had come to pass. He was gone.

Chapter Thirteen

I spent the next few days in my bed. I couldn't bring myself to care about anything. My only thoughts were on the love of my life who had disappeared. I cursed myself for making that wish. I cursed him for breaking a promise. I cursed the universe for taking him from me. I hated everyone and everything, and I could not figure out how life was supposed to go on.

My entire body ached from not moving. My stomach twisted, begging me to find some sustenance, but I had no strength and no will. My life was over. More than once, I had searched the apartment for pills of any kind, kicking myself for having the hospice nurse take all the leftovers. I wanted the all-encompassing pain to stop. I was drowning in grief and I wanted to put an end to it all.

There was nothing left for me in this life. I had estranged myself from my father. My love had been stolen from me. There would never be another man like Callum. Not just a genie, he was my soul mate. Why wasn't I his? The thought of him with someone else churned my stomach, but I had thrown up so many times already there was simply nothing left. The food in the apartment had all gone bad, and I couldn't bring myself to replenish it. People had come to the door more than once, but I never answered. I couldn't handle their questions and their sympathetic eyes.

"Care to explain this mess, little sprite?"

It wasn't the first time I had heard his voice in these lonely days. It was as if my subconscious tried to fool me into snapping out of my depressed stupor. Rolling over in bed, I covered my head with the pillow.

The pillow was torn from my fingers, scaring me so much I rolled off the side of the bed. Jumping up, I turned to see a man standing in my bedroom. Not just any man. Callum. But he was different, his skin the color of smooth golden oak and his hair brown with perfect blonde highlights. I almost didn't recognize him, but for his eyes. I would never forget those eyes.

"C-C... No. It can't be. You disappeared! You've been gone for days!"

"It's me, little sprite. I'm so sorry it took so long for me to return to you. I didn't know exactly what would happen. No one ever told me. But I'm here now, and I will never leave your side again.

My entire body trembled, and my heart beat so fast it made me dizzy. My vision darkened, and I felt myself fall, but the impact never came.

Waking up in my bed, I knew I wasn't alone. I heard a chair scrape the floor and turned to meet the deep-purple eyes that had haunted my dreams.

"God, I missed you," he admitted, running the back of his hand gently down my cheek.

I pressed hard against his touch. I needed to know he was really there. I needed to feel his warmth and his strength. I would not survive another torturous dream. "I had so many dreams. Promise me you aren't a dream. Promise me!" The last two words came out in a pleading sob.

Pulling the covers from my body, he scooped me into his arms and held me tightly against his chest. "It's me, sprite. I swear it's me. What can I do? How can I prove it?"

My entire body shook, and I could not get close enough to him. "I need to feel you. I need to feel all of you, Please."

Laying me down, he shucked his clothing and crawled on top of me, covering my body with his own. He kissed the tear tracks from my eyes all the way down to my chin before nuzzling into my neck.

Frantically, I shimmied out of my own clothing and wrapped my arms around him. My nipples stood at attention as he rubbed his chest against me. His lips trailed down over my collarbone and chest but avoided the sensitive peaks. Boldly, I wrapped my fingers in his hair and attempted to guide his mouth to where I needed it the most. Peeling out of my grasp, he regarded me for a moment before lifting his hand and snapping his fingers. I sucked in a deep breath, but before I could do anything, my hands were bound above my head. "But, how?" I asked as I tugged on the rope.

"Seems as long as I behave myself and follow the rules, I get to keep a few of my tricks." He winked.

"Rules aren't my thing," I sassed.

"Don't worry. I know how to keep your snarky little butt in line, don't I?"

The veiled threat sent a shiver down my spine. I knew I could keep pushing and get exactly what I wanted. "I don't know about that. You've been gone so long, I think you may have forgotten."

"Is that how you want to play this?" He raised a brow at me, and I bit my lip in reply as I turned away from his knowing gaze. "Sprite, look at me," he commanded.

Closing my eyes tight, I turned back and took a deep breath before doing as he asked.

"Good girl. Now, if you want a spanking, I would be happy to oblige, but I want to hear you ask for it."

"What?" I screeched. He'd never made me ask before. He was in charge. He decided what was what. I didn't need to ask because he always just knew.

"I want you to ask me to spank you." he repeated.

"But why? We never did that before!" I exclaimed as I tried to wiggle away from him.

"Stop throwing a tantrum and listen to me," he barked. Surprised, I fell still and waited to hear what he had to say. "Good girl, thank you. Now, I told you I got to keep a few of my tricks, but not all of them. I can no longer tap into that mind of yours. While I don't believe this will be a long-term issue, I need to relearn a few things about you. We have always had a special bond, and I know what your body craves, but I need to hear you ask for it. I need to hear you are ready to submit to me in all things. I need you to tell me you will be my wife."

My eyes filled with tears and, as he continued to speak, I lost my breath. He had never asked me to submit to him, it had simply been something I did. He had spanked me when I deserved it. Always on his terms. But this was new and different. He was giving me some control. I wasn't sure I liked it.

"I want to submit. I want to be your wife. I need to."

"Then do as I have asked. Show me how badly you want it."

My chin quivered, and my voice shook with my embarrassment. "Will you please spank me, Sir?"

Leaning down, he kissed me gently. "That's my girl. Why do you need a spanking? Have you been naughty?"

"No, Sir!" I shook my head. "I-I need to feel the sting. I need to know you are here and what you are saying is true."

"That wasn't so hard now, was it?" My wrists released, I was pulled into his arms once more. Straddling his lap, I wished he had stripped himself completely. The bulge behind his boxers pressed against my heat. Well, *I just found the second perk of his being human.* "You are naughty. You don't get any of that until I make an honest woman out of you," he teased.

I reared back and looked him in the eyes. "You're joking right?"

"I have never been more serious."

"But, we basically have had sex already. What's the difference?" I couldn't help my pitiful whine. I wanted him, and I wanted him now.

"That was then, this is now, and I'm sorry, little sprite. I'm kind of old-fashioned in that way."

I let my forehead drop to his shoulder. "Ugh! you are so frustrating!"

"Yes well, it's about to get worse." Flipping me stomach down, he situated me for my spanking.

"No! No no no! If you aren't going to fuck me, you don't get to spank me!" I kicked and yelled.

Callum chuckled, "Oh is that right? Well, if that was the case a few seconds ago, it is certainly not the case now. Have you developed a dirty mouth again so soon?"

I hadn't realized what I'd said until he pointed it out. "Oops." I covered my eyes. "I didn't mean it like that! It's just another word for sex! Come on! It's different."

"It most certainly is not different. I have told you more than once I dislike the use of vulgar words. You have been punished for it multiple times. I am now making it my mission this will be the final time we discuss this."

I gulped. This was not good. When Callum had a mission, nothing could stop him from pursuing it. I had learned that in my very first encounter with him. "I'm sorry, Sir. Please don't punish me."

"Do you want to submit to me, little sprite?" I nodded without a thought. "Then you have earned this punishment. You need to know I will always follow through with my promises." he announced before the first stinging swat found my backside.

Epilogue

My heart pounded, and my palms were sweating as I stood staring at myself in the mirror. My simple knee-length white dress floated around me, making me feel like I could lift off the ground at any moment. Of course, it might have been my mood. The day had finally come when I was going to marry my genie. He wasn't technically a genie anymore, but he still managed to make all of my dreams come true and then some. Callum was still getting acclimated to life as a human. It cracked me up every time he tripped on something or complained about wearing clothes. I tried to get him to agree to a "clothing optional" lifestyle, but the stubborn man wanted to wait for our special night for the big reveal. He thought pretty highly of himself, for sure.

Picking up my flowers, I took one last look at myself. Six months before I would have laughed in the face of anyone who told me how my life was going to end up, but now I could not imagine anything better. Well, not completely true. I picked up the framed photo of my mother I always kept close. Her smiling eyes and snarky grin were all the reminder I needed of the woman I now proudly called Mom. "I wish you were here," I choked out. "I am so thankful for everything you did for me. You changed my life, gave me a purpose, taught me how to love and trust. I promise to keep living in a way that makes you proud." A chuckle came through my emotion laced monologue. "We both know Callum won't let me stray too far."

Grabbing a tissue, I dabbed my tears gently as to not smudge my makeup. I kissed the photo before setting it down next to me. I had decided to carry it down the aisle with me. Mom deserved to be a part of our special day.

After one last deep breath, I left the office of the shop and stepped onto the white runner placed at the mouth of the hall. The whole town had showed up to witness Callum and I getting married. We had told them all he was a boyfriend from back home who had been tying up loose ends before he could join me here. I teased him mercilessly about lying, but we had no other explanation. He had been my boyfriend, of sorts, and he was from my home. This was my home. My real home. I still loved the city, but that life was not for me anymore. I was the owner and operator of an amazing store that attracted tourists from all over. The online store also boomed. People loved the unique things that could only be found in a place like this, and being able to shop from the comfort of their own homes made it even better.

Callum helped a lot in the store also, but he was more apt to choose the domestic chores. His cooking skills surpassed his customer service. Although, after his last debacle with the washing machine, he was no longer allowed to touch the dirty clothes.

One foot in front of the other until I could finally turn the corner and lay eyes on my man. He had been able to conjure up his own tuxedo to my specifications, and it fit him like a glove. The jacket hugged his broad muscled chest, and his red bow tie matched the blood-red of my roses. I made him promise me that after the ceremony and reception, he would model the bow tie for me, only the bow tie. My eyes landed on his, and the emotion I saw there took my breath away. I could not imagine loving someone as much as I loved him, nor could I imagine being loved by anyone else the way he loved me. We were wholly and truly soul mates.

Kicking off my shoes, I fell backward onto the bed. "Holy crap, that was a fun day, but I'm exhausted."

Callum joined me, having already unbuttoned the top of his dress shirt during the reception. "You'd better rest up, because I have plans for that delectable body of yours, and none of them include sleeping," he growled in my ear.

My pussy spasmed at the promise. I had been ready for him for days, so it didn't matter how tired I was, there was zero way I was going to sleep until he fed my need. I turned into him and wrapped my arms around his neck. "Are you going to let me sleep in tomorrow?" I teased, placing little kisses on his nose and around his mouth.

Grabbing my chin, he gazed at me, eyes hungry with lust. "You will be lucky if I let you out of bed at all for the next few days."

"Yes, Sir," I purred.

"Good girl. Let's get you out of this dress. It looks uncomfortable."

It wasn't, and he knew it wasn't. I had specifically chosen a comfortable dress because I couldn't imagine spending the day in something bulky and heavy. Standing up, he pulled me off the bed with him. I waited for him to make my clothing disappear. It was one of his favorite talents, but he stood staring at me for a moment.

"Turn around," he commanded in a low tone.

I obeyed, and he slowly lowered the zipper of my dress. He had never disrobed me this way before. I squirmed as the zipper gently scraped down my spine. Reaching the top of my ass, he ran his fingers up toward my shoulders and carefully slid the straps down my arms. I didn't move. His touch had me in a trance. Each touch sent zaps of pleasure throughout my entire body.

"Are you cold, little sprite?" he asked, nipping at my bare shoulder.

"No, Sir."

"Then why are you shivering?" He chuckled, and I almost turned around to kick him in the shin.

"You know why!" I pressed back against him, hoping he would continue his mission. He didn't disappoint. His hands came over my shoulders and toward my breast. I sucked in a breath as his knuckles grazed my nipples.

"Is this what you want, my beautiful bride?"

"This and so much more, my handsome husband." I reached back and grabbed hold of his erection through fabric of his dress pants, giving a small yank.

Hissing, he nipped my ear. "Behave, or I won't let you play," he threatened.

Feeling bold I turned around and hooked my fingers in his belt loops. "Please, Daddy, may I play with my new toy?" I purred. "I have been such a well-behaved little girl."

The purple of his eyes brightened, a look I had never seen before. Most of our relationship, he was only able to pleasure me. Since he had come back, he would not allow me any access to his manhood, but the torture ended tonight. I was going to feel my husband for the first time, and I absolutely could not wait.

~

Lying on my side, I appraised the glorious view of my

husband. He had fallen asleep with his hands behind his head, and I wanted to run my tongue around the contours of each muscle. I used my foot to pull the sheet farther down his body, revealing his massive erection. It called to me in a way I could not deny. I didn't want to. His breath was still deep and even. I almost bad for waking him up, but only for a second. Getting up on my knees, I crawled between his legs. I kissed the tip of his cock and looked up to see if he had woken. His eyes remained closed, but his smirk on his lips. Two could play at that game. I opened my mouth wide and took him deep inside. When he bumped the back of my throat, he could not keep his pleasure to himself. A low groan came from his chest as his eyes met mine. The sparkle of his deep-purple eyes encouraged me to go on. I had never enjoyed giving head to any man, but he was my husband, and all I wanted to do was bring him pleasure. It didn't hurt he tasted divine. I worked his cock with my mouth, listening to his small moans of satisfaction. I homed in on what he liked and what he didn't pretty quickly. Taking him to the back of my throat again I swallowed him whole. His hands came to the side of my head, preventing me from moving. I held my breath, doing my best not to gag or panic. Callum would never use his power to hurt me. I kept my eyes on his, and his smile gave me strength. Letting me go, he put his hands back behind his head. I sat up for a moment and wiped the spit from my mouth.

"Why don't you climb up here?" he coaxed.

I liked that idea, but he had given me so much pleasure I was determined to repay him. "Not yet." I shook my head and went back to business. This time, I worked him hard, not letting up until his body tensed and he came down my throat.

Crawling back up the bed I made myself comfortable

on his chest as he basked in the afterglow. The room smelled of sex and sweat, it did nothing to quell my lust. I had never felt so insatiable.

He wrapped his arm around me and lifted me onto his chest so we were face to face. “You defied me, little girl.”

I bit my lip. “But you liked it.”

“I did, however ,we both know I can’t let you get away with being so naughty, now, can we?”

I shrugged, not knowing what he had in mind. I didn’t want a spanking. My ass still ached from the night before.

“Now you climb up here and do as you were told.” He lifted me into place, and I welcomed his cock into my pussy. I couldn’t help the shudder of excitement as his erection scraped against every part of my core. I ground against him, trying to cause some friction to my clit. His body was made specifically for me and I planned to enjoy it as much as I could for the rest of our lives.

He smiled menacingly as he watched me search for my pleasure. “There is only one catch, little sprite. You are not allowed to come.”

THE END

Also by Allysa Hart

A Rose in Bloom

"You are not just my wife, you are my world."

Keith and Rose have been happily married for years, but when they begin their journey to build a family they are thrown into a tailspin of disappointment and they begin to lose each other and themselves.

After months of growing apart, Keith makes the decision to reclaim his wife and whisks her off to an exclusive

BDSM resort. Rawhide Ranch had come highly recommended as a place for lifestyle couples to congregate and play out their fantasies. But upon arrival, they realize there is a lot more to the ranch than meets the eye.

Keith and Rose aren't quite sure what to do about their discovery, but a vacation is a vacation and they decide to embrace the experience and all it has to offer. What they find opens up a whole new world and a journey they could have never foretold.

Adopting Katie

"If you ever put yourself in danger like that again, I will take you over my knee and spank your little bottom until I am convinced you have learned your lesson… How does that promise make you feel? Because make no mistake about it, Baby, it is definitely a promise."

A successful CEO by day, Katelyn looks forward to the minute she crosses the threshold to shed all of her adulthood stress and worries and become a carefree, mischievous little mess maker. Her husband and Daddy, Mark, is one of the most beautiful people, inside and out, that she has ever met. His dominance turns all of her switches, but she learns quickly that he means what he says and testing Daddy is not in her backside's best interest.

Mark is not alone in his endeavor to create a safe and loving environment for Katie. His best friends, Keith and Rose, round out their little family. Being intimately familiar with alternative lifestyles, the couple love and spoil Katie in abundance, but never think twice about turning her bottom red if she steps out of line.

Surrounded by her loving Daddy and adoring Auntie and Uncle, Katie learns that the love, safety, and guidance of this family are what help to make her feel complete.

Exploring the little girl who lives inside, the one that she has hidden for far too long, she spends her time building elaborate Lego structures and playing in her special tree house that Mark built by hand.

When tragedy strikes, Katie's idyllic life is shattered and it takes all of the love, support, and discipline of her family to pick up the pieces and put them back together. However, will love and spankings be enough? Katie is not convinced. She doesn't believe anything will ever be okay again.

About The Author

Meet Allysa Hart and Allycat's Creations!

I am a full-time mom to a sassy, strong-willed, loveable little girl. Okay, so she is all me. I am on the wrong side of 30, and I have been married to my best friend for over eight years. Like most couples, we have our ups and downs, but I could not imagine doing life with anyone else by my side. We are Southern California transplants, currently residing in a very rural part of the east coast. I have two crazy dogs that I adore, even though they drive me out of my ever-loving mind, most days.

I have recently rediscovered my love of words and decided to become a writer. My first story is my heart and soul, and it reaches into the depths of all that is me. I also create covers, promos, and logos for authors. I have met some amazing friends on this journey that I now happily call family. Without my family members, whether biological or chosen, I would not be half the person I am today. Their constant love and support keep me afloat.

Be sure not to miss anything by signing up for my *Newsletter*
Follow me on Facebook
Follow me on BookBub
Check out my Blog

CPSIA information can be obtained
at www.ICGtesting.com
Printed in the USA
LVHW011525010320
648615LV00004B/880